Fifties Chix: Broken Record

Angela Sage Larsen

13-1208

Published by Premiere

For my brother, Ryan.
Even if we weren't related, you'd be my soul brother and a good friend;
you continue to inspire me, make me laugh, and make me think.
And for my adorable, way-above average nephews: Bryce, Parker, Joel, William, and
Nicolas.
Love you boys.

ॐ

Acknowledgments

First and foremost, I must acknowledge my husband, best friend, business partner, personal assistant and cheerleader, the papa of Fifties Chix, Whit Larsen. If he were the only person I had to thank, I would be blessed beyond measure ... but there are multiple amazing individuals on my list! My extraordinary publishing team, including Lori Van Houten, Liz Wallingford, Bruce Butterfield, Marie Stroughter, Mariena Foley, Matt O'Grady, and everyone at FastPencil PREMIERE. I'd like to acknowledge my girlfriends who are so full of love and light just their presence makes the world a better place. Fifties Chix readers, you feel like family; thanks for taking this journey with me! And to my *other* family, especially my parents and parents-in-law, I hope you know that the best way I can express my gratitude for you is by writing these books.

Contents

Prologue

"The future belongs to those who believe in the beauty of their dreams."

—*Eleanor Roosevelt*

1

Boys on the Side

I DON'T LIKE MY MOM. THERE IT IS. I SAID IT.
SURE, I LOVE HER AND ALL . . . SHE IS MY MOM.
BUT I DON'T LIKE HOW SHE MAKES MY DAD
FEEL. THAT'S WHY I CHOSE TO STAY WITH HIM
WHEN SHE MOVED TO NEW ORLEANS. SHE
MAKES EVERYTHING INTO A BIG DRAMATIC DEAL
AND I HATE DRAMA. I MISS MY LITTLE BROTHER
AND SISTERS, BUT THEY ADD DRAMA AND SEE
ABOVE WHAT I THINK ABOUT THAT.

I FEEL BETTER JUST WRITING THIS DOWN,
LIKE MRS. F SAID. I GUESS I THOUGHT IT WAS
KINDA LAME WHEN SHE TOLD ME I SHOULD KEEP
A JOURNAL. WHEN I GOT SUSPENDED FOR

PULLING THE FIRE ALARM, SHE SAW HOW ANGRY I WAS. SHE WAS COOL ABOUT IT. SHE DIDN'T PRY OR ANYTHING, SHE JUST SAT BY ME IN THE OFFICE AFTER SCHOOL WHILE I WAITED TO TALK TO PRINCIPAL JONES AND THEN SHE SAID THERE'S MORE PRODUCTIVE WAYS OF GETTING YOUR FEELINGS OUT AND THAT'S WHEN SHE TOLD ME THE JOURNAL IDEA. I LIKE MRS. F AND ALL, BUT I THOUGHT NO WAY IS THAT EVER GOING TO HAPPEN. "I CAN'T THINK OF ONE GUY I KNOW THAT KEEPS A JOURNAL," I TOLD HER. THEN I THOUGHT OF O'GRADY AND GARY JENKINS. I BET THEY DO, BUT I DIDN'T SAY IT. THEY'RE COOL ENOUGH, BUT I'M NOT LIKE THEM IN A LOT OF WAYS. ANYHOW, I TRIED IT THAT NIGHT AND I'VE BEEN DOING IT EVER SINCE. I FIGURE NO ONE WILL EVER READ IT, RIGHT? SO WHAT THE HECK. PLUS NOW I REALLY LIKE WRITING. MAKES ME TAKE COLLEGE MORE SERIOUSLY. AND I EVEN WROTE SOMETHING FOR JAMES'S PAPER FOR MAXINE, "THE VISIBLE TRUTH."

SO . . . MY MOM. I'M THINKING ABOUT HER A LITTLE MORE THAN USUAL —USUAL BEING

PRETENDING SHE DOESN'T EXIST— BECAUSE
DAD TOLD ME THAT SHE'S COMING INTO TOWN
TO SEE ME PLAY IN THE BIG GAME TODAY.
THANKS FOR THE NOTICE. I BET IT JUST HAS
NOTHING TO DO WITH ME AND MAXINE BOTH
GETTING SUSPENDED WITHIN A FEW WEEKS OF
EACH OTHER (LIKE I SAID . . . <u>DRAMA!!</u>).
    SEE YA NEXT TIME, SAME PLACE TOMORROW
NIGHT, HOPEFULLY AS DISTRICT CHAMPS.
  - PEACE OUT,

C.M.

Conrad Marshall shoved his top-secret journal into its usual spot under the back corner of his mattress. Not that it mattered; his dad TJ never went into his room. Conrad didn't give him reason to: the tiny room in their two-bedroom place was spotless, just like the rest of the sparsely furnished apartment. In some ways, it was cool being a bachelor with TJ. But in most ways, Conrad missed the warmth and bustle (the activity but *not* the *drama*) of a family. Missing it this morning, he grabbed his backpack and headed for Maxine's, eager to commiserate with his cousin on the way to school about the news of his mom coming to town. Escorting her back to school after her unjust suspension wouldn't be such a bad thing, either.

Gary Jenkins
AP World History
Mrs. Fairview

UNSTABLE GROUNDS

The Balkans suffered through a decade of wars in the 1990s, in what is little known as the deadliest conflict in Europe since World War II. The resulting unstable "peace," the recognition of new and separate sovereign territories, has left the region economically and emotionally depressed. What? Like Mrs. F is going to treat this paper seriously if I say the Balkans are "emotionally depressed." How am I supposed to know? History books don't tell you diddly squat about what it's really like. No one talks about those wars and conflicts in former Yugoslavia. It's weird actually, maybe it's a conspiracy. Didn't I hear that Ann's parents are from Belgrade? It would be another excuse to

Delete. Delete. Delete. Delete. Gary Jenkins held his finger on that well-used key and erased all but the first sentence and sighed. Bob's music was pounding in the next room and he wished he could blame his lack of concentration on the shuddering wall between him and his brother, but he frankly hadn't noticed until this moment. He stretched and took a deep breath. This was his last big project before the end of the school year. Uncharacteristically, he just wanted it done with so he could enjoy the end of the year festivities. But this paper for AP History for Mrs. Fairview was wiping him out.

It didn't help that his mind wandered to Ann Branislav every other moment. He never thought he'd fall for one of his little sister's friends. First, because he thought it was kinda creepy; and b), because until befriending Ann, Bev typically only hung out with jock types, which was to say, not Gary's type.

He was crazy to think he could get anything done before school anyway. He'd hoped to come up with a valid thesis statement at least. The rest, he told himself, like actually finding out more about the Balkans, was cake.

Does Ann like cake?

It was going to be a long day.

Even through the throbbing music and sweet bass line, Bob could hear his phone—across the room and muffled by his unmade bed—vibrate with an incoming message. He promised himself he'd finish his reps—ten more thirty-pound curls and then he'd check the text. But he knew who it was from. Diane texted him day and night. Bob thought there should be a law: you just don't text before school starts or after midnight unless you're leaving a party. It just seemed weird. He wasn't going to be in the mood to text her back which would result in a fight, or worse—her annoying passive-aggressive comments that would leave him perplexed and feeling stupid. Was there that much to say that her thumbs had to be skittering across her phone every waking (and should-be-sleeping) moment?

Still, she was cute and a star athlete, and Bob had to admit he didn't mind the attention from the other guys that dating Diane got him.

Heaving one last breath and rep, he carefully set down the dumbbell, remembering the dent he'd once made in his wall with his weights and his mom's anger when she'd seen it. Mopping his face, he grabbed his phone.

Morning sunshine. guess what? North out of tournament…that means we're in!!! omg!

Bob couldn't help himself. He usually purposely did not write her back before school, trying to prove to Diane that he just never looked at his phone, but this time he had to respond.

U mean girls softball back in?? he wrote.

Thats what I'm telling you. and if we had your sister play with us we could even win it all. DO NOT TELL HER I SAID THAT.

Bob snorted. He knew better than to talk about Diane with his sister Bev about anything, but especially when it came to sports. If it was possible, Bev was more competitive than even Bob was. Besides, he wouldn't mention it to Bev in case she *was* tempted to leave the guys' team and go play with the girls. They had district quarterfinals and the team was just getting adjusted to Bev and they were in a groove. He realized how totally unfair it was that Bev could play with either team. *He* didn't have the choice of playing with the girls' softball team. He snorted again.

Tossing his phone back down, he headed for the shower to get ready for school. He didn't like being at Diane Dunkelman's beck and call—or in this case, beck and text. He'd already agreed not to contribute to the literary protest his friends had organized when Conrad's cousin, Maxine, had been suspended.

Diane had told Bob all about it, how Maxine had posted a threat online and written some racist article. Bob, of course, had immediately rushed to read the essay with great interest. Not. But he'd agreed to stay out of the fray with *The Visible Truth* not just because he wasn't particularly interested in doing extra schoolwork for zero credit, but also because it would appease Diane. At least momentarily.

He wondered, not for the first time, if appeasing her constantly was really worth it.

James O'Grady flipped through his fresh copy of *The Visible Truth* for possibly the millionth time. It was the perfect way to end the year. It was clever, ironic, and more than that, it was social commentary and a non-violent protest to the ridiculous suspension Maxine Marshall had been dealt for either something she hadn't done (used Facebook to threaten to bring a gun to school), or for something she *had* done (written the essay called "Useless Generation") that didn't deserve punishment.

He still wanted to write that article about Twigler, the mysterious school custodian, but with only a week and a half of school left, *The Visible Truth* would have to be his last underground publication for the year. James was proud of his instincts about wanting to write about Twigler, though: he'd had a hunch there was more to the old man than met the eye, and James had been right. He'd discovered that Thomas Twigler had had a high-paying, top-secret government contract researching time travel.

That was right up James's alley. If he wasn't planning on being a journalist, he'd be the first in line to be in an über-secret government agency to find out if time travel really was possible. And maybe answer some questions for Mary Donovan and her friends, too.

Except that he already had his answer. It was not only possible, it was happening right under his nose. Mary and her friends had obviously shown up from the 1950s with their old-fashioned attitudes, clothing, and sensibilities. It was so disarming that ever since those first few conversations with Mary, he'd been feeling as if he was watching his own life roll out in front of him like wire unwinding off a big cosmic spool. What was real, what was imagination, and was any of it a result of his own doing, or was it all random? Mundane events in his day fascinated him. Were they signs? Where they illusions? Was he a visitor here from another dimension? Either Mary was time traveling, or he was, or they all were. It was a constant effort to calm his nerves and not jump the gun or spook Mary with his eagerness to figure it all out. He trod carefully; he didn't want to hurt her . . . or anyone else.

Including his parents. James's stomach lurched as he thought of the upcoming family court visit. Because his dueling parents demanded he choose whom to live with when their divorce was final and he refused to decide, he was required to meet with a judge in private and discuss the issue—on a Saturday, no less. James found it embarrassing, frankly, that his parents were so bull-headed that they couldn't just agree to joint custody. He hadn't told a soul just how badly things had deteriorated between his mom and dad and, as result, between him and his parents. The divorce itself, which his close friends knew about, wasn't so terrible; but it was his being used as a human pawn by his parents to get back at each other that pained him.

He planned on telling the judge he wanted to live with his Aunt Row. His parents would hate it, but hopefully Aunt Row wouldn't mind.

Talking to the O'Grady kid got Tommy Twigler thinking about Rowena Nolan all over again. He'd spent a lifetime trying to forget her. He didn't try that hard; he was still living practically right around the corner from her. He had been convinced that when she married and had six rugrats, it would be easy enough to let go. He hadn't considered that she'd never marry. What a waste. The moments he allowed himself to wonder if it had anything to do with him were swiftly followed with a self-deprecating rebuke that he had some ego to think he'd made any kind of an impression whatsoever on Row.

Part of his fascination with Row had certainly begun in high school when, in the span of one weekend, she became another person. Something had happened with her two friends, too; Reggie's now-wife, May, and that dancer, Emily Jackson. Twig remembered when it was, right around Thanksgiving, because a month later—Christmas—Emily had vanished. There were rumors she'd run off to New York to dance or that she'd joined the circus. Either of them could have been plausible if it weren't that all three girls had been acting differently, like they'd all had a mutual life-changing experience. Like finding a body or covering up a crime or some such thing.

Not that he'd ever think the girls were criminals, but Twig had suspected that if it had something to do with a crime, it was the theft of a solid gold watch. The first week in December, 1945, he'd been working in his foster dad's clock shop and watched May Boggs pace back and forth on the street for a half an hour before coming in. She'd been flushed, anxious.

Without any pleasantries or greeting whatsoever, she'd said, "What do you know about time?"

It was a strange question. "You mean keeping time, like watches and clocks? I can fix timepieces," he'd answered, feeling somehow that he'd missed her meaning.

May had stared at him, but not really looking at him at all. She had been thinking, trying to decide something. Before, Twig had had a hunch that May was a bit sweet on him and therefore intimidated by him, but the way she'd gazed right through him then, he might as well have been invisible.

"Is there something you want me to take a look at?" Twig had asked. He was starting to feel uncomfortable, hoping someone else would walk in the shop so they wouldn't be alone.

"I really shouldn't."

"Suit yourself. You came in here, remember?"

Suddenly May had perked up, as if something had occurred to her. "Do you have antique watches, maybe from Europe? Gold? You know, something *really* special."

"To buy? Well, I'm not supposed to take things out of the safe . . . ."

"Oh, please, Tommy. I'm sorry I'm acting like an oddball, truly. Can you at least tell me about any watches you have like that? Do they do anything special?"

Twig had laughed. "Well, they tell time. That's special enough, I guess."

Slowly, May had pulled one hand out of her skirt pocket, where it had been firmly planted since she'd walked into the shop. "I'm looking for something like—"

"Hey there, Tommy! Tell your pops we got fresh eggs if he wants 'em." Artie, the mail man, had saluted Twig with a packet of mail as he'd swung open the door. He'd then laid it on the counter.

"Sure thing, Artie." Twig waved goodbye to the postman and turned back to May. But she'd been spooked. Twig had only caught a glimpse of the gold watch she'd been clutching but was now back in her pocket.

"Well, I don't think I need anything. I'll come back if I do." May had scurried for the door. Before walking out, she'd turned and said very seriously, "Thanks for your help, Tommy. Sorry I'm acting like an oddball. Don't tell anyone I came in, OK? Not Row or Em?"

"Whatever you say."

Though Twig had given her a friendly wave, the whole incident stuck in his craw. In ten years, he hadn't forgotten a single detail of May's visit to the shop. His mind was like that; it was a blessing and a curse, as they say. He never forgot a face or a name, or even a date. Which is why a decade later, in 1955, when Row Nolan herself brought the watch in to be fixed, he knew it was the same one. And . . . he knew it was why he'd been recruited to help Reggie Fairview with his special government project. His whole life had been intertwined with Row's whether she liked it or not . . . and he had nothing to show for it.

2

Sour Grapes

"Daddy!" May Boggs scrambled through the front door of her own house, screaming more frantically than she'd meant to. After leaving Row's house, she had run the whole way to her own, marveling at the changes to her and Row's neighborhoods now in 1945. Still exhausted and bewildered, she felt just as desperate for answers as the morning she'd woken up in 1864 a mere few weeks ago.

"What in the world . . . ?" May's mom sprang up from the kitchen floor, which she was dutifully scrubbing on her hands and knees like she did every Saturday morning. She ran to her daughter, the sudsy rag in her hand leaving a wet trail into the living room where May had rushed in.

May grabbed her mother and clung to her, not realizing how much she had missed her mom and her home, where everything familiar was predictably—blissfully—in place. The well-known details of her present day life looked oddly modern compared to where she'd just come from: the Civil War.

Into her mother's soft neck, May murmured, "I'm sorry I missed Thanksgiving."

Justine Boggs gave her daughter a squeeze and then pulled back sharply, asking, "What are you talking about, Marion? You had a one-night sleepover at Row's. Thanksgiving is next week. Now what is all this fussing about?"

"I need to talk to Daddy is all," May said, drying her eyes. She hadn't realized that the sight of her mother had driven her to tears.

"Marionberry," her dad said, as if on cue. He came from the hallway, straightening his suspenders. "How was the sleepover at Rowena's?"

May nearly knocked him over as she rushed to hug him.

"I need to talk to you, Dad," she said, holding him even tighter than her mother.

"Talk away," he laughed, trying to get air into his lungs through her unrelenting embrace.

"Just . . . us," she said.

"Oh, for crying out . . . ." Mrs. Boggs made a big dramatic sigh and went back into the kitchen and then made disgruntled sounds when she saw the mess she'd made with the soaking cloth dripping everywhere.

"I need to ask you about the family heirlooms you showed me that were under your bed," May whispered. "Especially the watch."

Her dad turned serious quickly. "Remember, now, you're not supposed to know about those things."

"I know. But I have questions. About your family's watch."

"That watch isn't my family's, Marion. It's your mother's."

❖   ❖   ❖

"I don't know what you think happened to it, but it's right here." Mr. Boggs held up the watch for May to see.

The color drained from May's face and her mouth formed an O. Standing in her parents' bedroom, facing her dad who had retrieved the watch from its normal place under her parents' bed, she didn't see her mom walk in behind her.

"Harold!" Mrs. Boggs barked. Both May and her dad jumped. "That is not a toy."

"Do you know about this watch? About what it can do?" May said, whipping around to face her mother and ignoring the tone of her mother's voice. May also ignored—for the moment—the complete impossibility that the watch could be in her father's hand, when she'd traded it to bounty hunters for the freedom of two slave women and an infant; when had that been? Yesterday or eighty-one years ago?

"Of course I know what it can do. It tells time. Harry, put it back in the box. It's a family heirloom and it's worth a great deal."

Mr. Boggs looked more closely at the watch and made a soft "Hmmm" sound.

"It doesn't tell time," May argued.

"Certainly not if you broke it!" said Mrs. Boggs.

Mr. Boggs turned the watch over in his hand. "I didn't realize it was inscribed," he said, mostly to himself.

"It's German," May and her mother said in unison, and then Mrs. Boggs pushed past May and lunged for her husband, snatching the watch from his hand. "I'm very disappointed in you two," she said. "Now I need to find a place to keep it safe from both of you."

Mr. Boggs laughed gently at his wife. "Safe? Justine, just what do you think —" But Mrs. Boggs was gone, having exited in a huff.

May and her dad stood staring at each other for a moment, trying to decide if they should follow Mrs. Boggs and beg forgiveness. But first, May had a question. "You speak German, don't you, Dad? What did the inscription say?"

"*I think it said:* Love cannot be contained by time. Love is forever."

May was conflicted. She knew now that the watch wasn't missing (or at least it wouldn't be when she found her mother's hiding place for it), but as far as Em and Row were concerned, it was lost in 1864. Em was still desperate to go back, but May couldn't bear the thought of that; not because of her own safety or comfort, but for Emily's. They had discovered that Em was the descendant of a child born to a female slave and a ruthless slavemaster. If Em believed the watch to be gone for good, then going back to the 1860s wouldn't be an issue. But there was another problem: May couldn't help but wonder where else the watch could take them. Even as she was still recovering from a traumatic midnight escape via the Underground Railroad, her curiosity was alive and kicking.

Two weeks later, as May listened to the radio shows with her mother after school, her mind wandered. She couldn't keep track of Dwight and Carolyn Kramer on "The Right to Happiness" and frankly had lost interest anyway. The story was contrived and artificial. She had been seeing everything in a new light. Previously unremarkable daily things had taken on a magical glow and May wondered about their story, while other things—and people, like Tommy Twigler—that used to interest her no longer appealed. She had briefly toyed with having the watch dissected and had even taken it to Twigler's foster dad's clock shop, but had thought better of it in the end. Not caring that she was interrupting the radio show, May spoke up.

"What makes that watch so special?" she blurted to her mother. May had hoped to find the perfect time and the perfect way in which to approach the subject so as not to turn her mother off the topic for good, but May didn't have the patience to wait a second longer. At school, Emily moped around, nervous and jumpy at any sudden sounds, and Rowena looked uncharacteristically worried. May had wondered if they should go back to 1864 and check on Emily's for-bears, if there was a chance it would bring the spark back to her friends' eyes.

"Shhh . . . I'm listening to your show," May's mother said as she polished the silver even though it had just been polished for Thanks-giving the week before.

May reached over and turned the radio off. Unthinkable a month ago. "It's not my show. And I don't care about the Kramers. I care about real life."

Outside, clouds were racing by, tumbling over each other and threatening to storm. Through the kitchen windows, shadows and light danced through the lace curtains, making dramatic patterns on Mrs. Bogg's simple but sparkling clean kitchen. The bare tree branches shimmied in the wind, some of their fingertips scratching the side of the house eerily. Though the radiator was on, Mrs. Bogg had opened the paned window over the sink just a crack for fresh air. She had been scrubbing with a vengeance and had worked up a sweat.

"Well, I only listen to those shows because—"

"Mother. Please. Tell me about that watch." May was not in the habit of interrupting her mother or being insolent toward her.

Her mom sighed, put down the silver, and straightened the kerchief she wore to cover her hair when cleaning. A strand of her auburn hair floated out near her temple. May looked at her as if seeing her for the first time. Her mother was just a woman doing the best she could. Just a person. May wondered why she had never quite seen that before. But her mother's life was so . . . dull; and it was as if Justine Boggs had chosen it that way on purpose. She could have worn her hair down in soft curls, laughed more (her husband was always trying to make her smile), gone out dancing like Row's parents, Mr. and Mrs. Nolan, used to do. Before Mrs. Nolan's heart had broken.

"I'm going to sell it," Mrs. Boggs said after a long pause.

May gasped. "No! You said it's a family heirloom and it's worth a fortune!"

"Precisely why we need to sell it. The war's over, I'm not working anymore, and we need to have money set aside for you when you get married and start a family of your own."

"Who says I'm getting married?" May shook her head. That was beside the point. "Mother, you cannot sell that watch. Especially not for me. If you want me to have something, then give me the watch."

"I just don't see how it's any of your concern, young lady." Mrs. Boggs reached for the radio to turn it back on, but May swatted her hand away and then gasped at her own audacity.

"Marion Gertrude!"

"I'm sorry," May apologized with all sincerity. But she wasn't giving up. "It's my family, too! Can you please just talk to me—"

"It was my grandmother's watch," Mrs. Boggs said in a rush, in a tone bordering on a shout. Then she regained her composure. "You didn't know your great-grandmother Marion, but you were named after her, did you know that?" Of course May knew. May remained silent, holding her breath and waiting for her mom to continue. She did: "Mamie Marion came to America to escape the unrest from the Franco-Prussian war. She had run away from home and was living in Paris as an actress; but when there was an uprising there after the war, she fled to St. Louis with just that watch to her name. Her family always treated her like an outcast. I suppose she was; she was an eccentric woman." A smile spread across Mrs. Boggs's face. "Oh, but I loved her. Her life was so full of adventure and she was so sure of herself. I wanted to be just like her when I was young."

May swallowed the words, Then why aren't you? But her mother must have read her mind.

"When you were just two, your great Mamie Marion died poor and alone. But that's not all; she spent her last days committed to a sanitorium. She had prattled on about the black plague and building cathedrals; she went on and on about having tea with Catherine the Great and fighting wars that were one hundred years before her time."

May's heart raced while the rest of the world stood still. This was the most her mother had ever confided in her and she didn't dare do so much as blink, lest her mother catch herself and clam up immediately.

"She had only one thing left. That watch. And she left it to me. Oh, was my mother angry that Mamie Marion had skipped right over her to give it to me. Only a month later our little Harry Jr. was born and died within a week." Now Mrs. Boggs looked her daughter in the eye. Tears glistened in her own. May never heard her mom speak of her baby brother.

Mrs. Boggs took a deep breath, as if to steady herself. "I do know what that watch does, Marion. It causes people to go insane."

3

No Big Deal

Judy White couldn't wait to eat lunch with her friends again, but it would have to be postponed a bit longer because she had an appointment to see Principal Jones and tell him about her discovery of Diane Dunkelman's plot to frame Maxine. She had chickened out of doing it yesterday. But upon seeing Maxine back in school this morning after her suspension, Judy had fresh courage. To make the day even better, she had noticed posters around school announcing auditions for a summer musical. She'd decided on the spot that she would audition for the lead. The only thing bugging her was that nagging little detail of her heartthrob Bob Jenkins not contributing to *The Visible Truth*. Judy made excuses for him, reminding herself of how busy he was with playoffs. That explanation, of course, held little water because Conrad, Bev, and two other baseball players had furnished pieces and had gone to see Maxine in person. Still, Judy reasoned, it was just further proof of how much Bob needed her.

As the bell rang to signal the start of lunch, she wriggled like a small fish against the current of big fish hustling to the cafeteria and parking lot and made her way to the office. As she crossed the last hall before reaching the glass-paned door of the office, she happened to glance down the locker-lined corridor and saw a single figure, hunched over and facing a corner.

Keep walking, a voice inside Judy's head urged, but what came out of her mouth was, "Diane?"

The figure turned quickly, straightened. Diane Dunkelman swiped tears from her face with her free hand; her other hand held her phone to her ear. She rolled her eyes at Judy, gesturing at the phone.

"OK, Sullie, it's not a big deal. I don't really care." She nodded to the voice on the other end and then said goodbye. She sniffled, but tried to hide it with attitude.

"Who was that?" Judy asked.

"My dad."

"You call your dad *Sullie*?"

"When I'm mad at him," Diane laughed, trying to play it off as a joke. Judy could tell Diane hadn't read Judy's piece in *The Visible Truth* yet; if she had, they wouldn't have been on speaking terms.

Again, the voice in Judy's head coaxed her to finish the conversation and move on, but her mouth disobeyed, asking, "Why are you mad at him?"

"This morning we just found out the softball team gets a shot at a big tournament this weekend because North was disqualified. I asked my *dad* to come to the games, but he's too *busy* with his *stupid girlfriend* and *her kid*." Diane emphasized the important words with contempt.

"Can't he just come to one game?" Judy asked lamely. This had the unfortunate effect of causing Diane to burst into tears. Real ones. Judy stood uncomfortably for an interval, looking around for someone to come to both their rescues, but there was no one. Judy moved closer to Diane and like a magnet, Diane draped herself over Judy in full-on bawl mode.

"Geez, it's not like I care, you know? It's like, what*ever*. Plus, we're not going to win anyway; we lost Bev to the—" Diane stopped herself from babbling.

Was she just about to somehow compliment Bev? Judy was stunned by this turn of events, trying to figure out if Diane had an angle or was really upset about the situation with her dad and Bev's not being on the girls' team anymore.

Judy tentatively patted Diane's back and searched for something comforting to say. "Maybe we can talk to her together," Judy said.

"Talk to who?"

Judy knew the voice before she let go of Diane and turned around. Bev stood with her hands on her hips, Ann next to her, arms crossed. By the expressions on their faces, they were pretty steamed to have found Judy with Diane. Especially when at this moment, Judy should have been inthe principal's office ratting out Diane.

"Oh, heya, Bev, Ann—" Judy started.

"Leave her alone," Bev huffed at Diane.

"She's not bothering me," Judy said. "We're just having a conversation."

"Do you need us to stick around?" Ann offered, hurling her best evil eye in Diane's direction.

As much as Judy appreciated her friends looking out for her, she assured them she was fine and would catch up with them later. They, like Judy herself, were wondering why Judy didn't just walk away from Diane right now after all Diane had done.

"Wow, so they totally hate me," Diane said. Judy turned back to her to see that Diane had pulled out a mirror and was cleaning up her eye makeup.

Suddenly Judy was annoyed with this roller coaster she'd been letting Diane take her for a ride on. "Well, what do you expect? You said terrible things about our friend, Maxine. And then you went and made a fake page online. We know it was you! She got suspended for that!"

"That was supposed to be a *joke*," Diane said defensively, not denying that she was behind it.

"Some joke. That was a real put-down. You really hurt people."

"If I'm so terrible, why have you been hanging out with me, then?" Diane challenged.

Judy didn't have a very good immediate answer. "Because . . . I . . . I knew that Maxine didn't make that page . . . . "

"So you were spying on me? You never even just came out and asked me. I would have told you."

Judy doubted that, but she didn't have a case; she had never intended to be Diane's friend and so was equally guilty of deceit. Which made her as bad as Diane herself. "If you're so happy to admit it, go tell Principal Jones," Judy challenged.

"Fine. I will."

"Fine. Do it."

The girls stood and glared at each other.

"Well, not *now*," Diane sneered. Her phone rang and without another word, she answered and walked away without excusing herself, leaving Judy standing in the hall alone, wondering what to do, about to get cold feet for the second day in a row.

When Bob rounded the corner and Diane skipped over to him and looped her arm around his neck, it was easy for Judy to decide.

"Hi, I'm here to see Principal Jones about an important matter," she told the school secretary thirty seconds later.

"I thought eventually things would get less weird," Ann said over lunch with Bev. She was eyeballing Diane Dunkelman hanging off of Bob's arm at the next table over. *Poor Judy.* Ann was glad Judy wasn't around to witness their latest display of couplehood.

"Which weird thing are *you* thinking about?" Bev asked. She had purposely sat with her back to Bob. She had a list of weird things on her mind.

"It still feels like we're strangers here, you know? And I feel even more like a stranger because my home country doesn't exist anymore. I mean, I know *this* is my home country. But it's a little odd to wake up and discover that Yugoslavia is no longer a place on the map."

Bev thought about that for a minute. She knew exactly what Ann meant. Bev's metaphorical home "country," you could say, wasn't on the map, either. Borders and boundary lines had been redefined and everything looked different. For example, in the

1950s, Ann's mom had been Bev's family's maid. Now their mothers were in business together, so occasionally, Bev got a glimpse of Mrs. B, but it wasn't the same. Bev missed her. She only occasionally got a glimpse of her own mom. And then there was going from playing for the girls' softball team with Diane Dunkelman to playing on the boys' team with Conrad Marshall. The false hope that maybe she could see Conrad socially outside of a baseball game was almost more painful than the knowledge in 1955 that that could never happen. It was *almost* more painful. . . .

"Can I tell you something if you swear to not tell the others?" Bev said. She blushed saying it. She wasn't one to gossip or bare her soul or share secrets or that kind of thing. But Ann, despite her dreamy artsy demeanor, was still possibly the most earthbound one among them at the moment.

Ann nodded.

"I don't know if I want to go back. You know," Bev whispered, "*to 1955*. Are we supposed to be trying?"

"Nobody would blame *you* for not wanting to go back," Ann said soothingly.

Alarmed, Bev said, "What do you mean?" Were her feelings for Conrad that obvious? Her brother Gary had already commented on it and said that even Bob had figured it out.

"Baseball," Ann said. "You get to play baseball. Why, where you thinking of something else?"

"No, nothing," Bev said.

Just then, the din of the overstuffed cafeteria was punctuated with the PA system: "Diane Dunkelman, please report to the principal's office. Diane Dunkelman to the principal's office."

"She did it!" Ann cried.

"Way to go, Judy," Bev enthused, grateful to have their conversation interrupted, especially by that.

"What will the softball team do without Diane Dunkelman now?" Ann wondered.

"Yeah," Bev laughed. Her belly did a little flip, thinking how fun it would have been to play softball without having to deal with Diane. But she was playing for the boys' team now, she reminded herself. And that was just as fun.

4

Play to Win

For the first time in her life, Maxine Marshall didn't feel alone. Well, for maybe the second time. Both times had been thanks to the Fifties Chix. Now back at school after her controversial suspension, and as the true story behind the Internet scandal spread, she was getting approving nods and encouraging signs from people she didn't know. She recalled a time in the not-too-distant past when she would have preferred to be invisible; but now, with all the unexpected attention, she realized that what she had *really* wanted was to be acknowledged in a positive way. She'd even gotten some respect in her own house, from her sister Mel, who was usually the chief attention-getter.

Maxine was glad to have walked to school with her cousin Conrad so he could see the favorable response she was getting. She knew he was worried about her; when she had written her essay "Useless Generation," he had ratted her out to Mel, who had been at college until a few days ago. Maxine couldn't be mad at Conrad, though; if he'd wanted to get her into trouble, he would have gone straight to her parents. He was obviously seeking big-sisterly advice from Mel.

Before they parted ways for class, Maxine said, "I"m sorry if my article made things hard between you and your friends."

"Aw, it's no thing," he said.

"What about Bob Jenkins?" she asked. She'd been wondering about him; Bob was friends with her cousin and the object of Judy's crush, and he was noticeably absent from the list of friends who'd contributed to writing an underground paper to honor Maxine. Maxine wasn't as concerned for herself as she was for Conrad and Judy.

"Bob's head's all messed up for Dunkelman." Conrad gave his cousin an affectionate chuck on the shoulder and they parted ways. Maxine adored Conrad, but he still felt like a stranger to her lately. Before, he'd been quieter, willing to fly below the radar. But now, he was bolder and brasher and she worried about him getting into trouble. Then she remembered that *she* was a bit bolder and brasher these days, too, and smiled to herself.

"Good to have you back," called Gary Jenkins as he walked by. She waved back.

"We've got to talk after school!"

Maxine jumped. Mary Donovan had appeared as if out of nowhere at her side. "Good to see you, too, Mary."

"Gee, I'm sorry, Maxine. Glad you're back at school, really. But we've got to get together. I think we're trapped here . . . in the *future*." Mary looked agitated, her face rosy with anxiety.

Before Maxine could suggest to Mary that maybe that wasn't such a bad thing, the bell rang and they had to sprint to class so they wouldn't be late.

Bev tried to contain her smug glee. Diane Dunkelman had been kicked off the girls' softball team for the rest of the season, as Ann had predicted, as a result of what Bev was told was "cyber-bullying." She had only recently learned what that meant, and if it got Diane to pay for giving her friends the royal shaft, then Bev was all for it. And the timing couldn't have been better: the softball team was going to participate in an important tournament over the weekend now that another school had been disqualified. Which is why the girls' coach had called Bev in after school and before warm-up for the boys' big game.

"The reason I called you in, Bev, is that, as you know, the team is really going to suffer with both you and Diane gone," Coach Rasmus said. "But there's more. Since spring softball isn't eligible for state playoffs, the tournament this weekend isn't about qualifying for state or advancing as a school team. Actually, it's a chance for scouts to come find talent. They are putting together a US girls' softball team to compete abroad in the fall. You are just the kind of competitive, talented player they're looking for."

Bev's smugness exploded into jubilation and she jumped out of the heavy wooden chair in front of Coach's desk. "Count me in, Coach! What do I need to do?" Her long-cherished dream of a playing on a women's league—though it wasn't baseball—was about to be realized in front of her eyes.

Coach's energy didn't match Beverly's. "It's not that simple, Jenkins. You win the quarterfinals with the boys tonight—and certainly, I hope you do—and you'll have to choose between playing in the tournament with the scouts *or* playing the semis and state finals with the boys. But you can't do both."

As quickly as Bev's hopes had rocketed sky-high, they crashed to the ground in flames. "But . . . . " Bev searched the far reaches of the universe for a way to be in two places at the same time. Maybe her knack for time travel could somehow come to her aid in this situation. "There's got to be a way . . . . " Yet she came up blank.

"I know it's a tough dilemma, but it's a pretty sweet one to be in, Jenkins. Not everyone has this kind of problem."

"Yeah," Bev agreed, dejected. She sat back down. This dilemma had a familiar feeling . . . it reminded her of liking someone, but not liking the *right* someone—at least according to everyone else.

"It won't be an issue if—"

"Don't even say it." Bev stopped Coach from reminding her that if the boys' team lost tonight, there would be no conflict for her on Saturday.

"I'm just saying, let's talk after the game tonight. If the option of playing with the boys is taken off the table, there's no issue. If a decision needs to be made, then we'll talk."

"Maybe the scouts could come see me play tonight?" Bev said.

"That would be nice, but it doesn't work that way this time."

Bev was annoyed at how matter-of-fact Coach Rasmus was, but she thought of her mom—her 1950s mom—and she stood up and put her hand out politely. "Thank you for thinking of me, Coach. And for all the ways you've helped me."

Coach was pleased, bordering on amused, and shook Bev's hand. "Go get 'em, Jenkins."

"We've got to make this snappy; I have a game to get ready for," Bev said. She tried to keep the irritation out of her voice. It wasn't her friends' fault, after all, that she had one too many great options in the future.

"Bev's right. Big game tonight!" Judy clapped excitedly. Bev gave her an appreciative smile, but she didn't feel the joy.

"Right." Mary took the reins of their meeting, as she so often did. "I'll cut to the chase. James talked to Twig and it turns out Mrs. F's watch broke . . . *in 1955.*"

"Who's Twig?" Bev asked.

"Mrs. F's watch?" said Ann.

"Twig is the custodian," Maxine offered. "But what does he have to do with anything?"

Once again, Judy's house played host to the friends, and they marveled that the central air conditioning they enjoyed at her house was common everywhere now. It would be another muggy evening outside, though, for Panthers baseball fans. Mary and the others were thankful that they could keep the windows closed when it was this hot, instead of trying to air out the room with fans and hoping for an outside breeze to blow through.

Judy and Mary would have liked to meet at the fifties diner again, but there wasn't enough time with Bev's schedule.

"Tom Twigler—the custodian—went to school with Mrs. F. At *our* school! In the forties. Look, I even found pictures of him." Mary had three yearbooks spread out in front of her, pages marked, and she turned them to the girls sitting across the table.

"He's a looker," Judy enthused. Maxine tried to not roll her eyes.

"The point is, he knows Aunt Row and Mrs. F; and Mrs. F— Miss Boggs, back then, I guess I should say—took her watch to him to be fixed." Mary further explained all the information she'd gathered from her conversation with James the evening before, including the fact that Twig's family had a clock repair shop.

"Wait a minute," Ann said more loudly than she'd intended. "I get that you're saying the watch had something to do with us time traveling . . . and we know that Miss Boggs and Aunt Row aged . . . but that means *Twig* did too."

Around the table, lights in eyes blinked on. "Ooooh," the girls sighed, intrigued.

"What does that mean?" Maxine puzzled out loud.

"I—I don't want to go back," Bev blurted. "If it was the watch, I'm glad it's broken."

Judy's cats, Dragnet and Desi, meowed loudly at the base of Judy's chair to be fed. "I don't know if I want to go back, either," Judy agreed.

"Now hold on," Maxine reasoned. She threw an annoyed glance at the disruptive cats. "Whether we want to go back or not, we don't even know if it's up to us—except that Mrs. F did tell us this *is* temporary. The issue is, if it is that watch, whether it's broken or not, we should have it. We should have the option of controlling our own destiny."

"Yes," agreed Bev, Ann, and Judy wholeheartedly.

Mary noticeably abstained.

"Do you agree, Mary?" Ann asked.

Mary couldn't sit still. Like she had when James had told her about Twig and the watch, she got up and paced the room. "I wonder if after all this, it would be that simple. Mrs. F hasn't given the watch to us voluntarily so far, and what are we supposed to do, *steal* it from her?"

"Why don't we just ask nicely?" Judy suggested.

"Can we wait to rock the boat until Sunday?" Bev said. "I've got bigger fish to fry."

"Of course, the game!" Ann put in.

"There's more," Bev clarified. She told them about her conflicting opportunities with the girls' and boys' teams over the weekend.

"But," Judy said, thinking out loud, "if you lose tonight—"

"Don't you dare say it, Judy White!" Bev interrupted and they all saw her meaning.

"There's no question; she's got to play with the *girls* tomorrow," Ann said, and Maxine agreed.

"But what about her loyalty to her own brother Bob and her team?" Judy argued.

"And the fact that she committed to the boys' team and they're where they are thanks to her," added Mary.

"I'm right here," Bev reminded them as they referenced her in third person. She thought of the conversations she'd overheard her parents having in the 1950s when they didn't know she was listening. Her mother, desperate for Bev to not play sports so that she wouldn't get hurt or appear unladylike; her pops at a loss for what to think about a girl wanting to play sports. Sometimes he'd treated her like one of her brothers. But Bev didn't want to *be* a boy. She wanted to be a girl who was a good athlete.

"Well, play your heart out tonight, no matter what," Ann said.

"Yeah, follow your heart," said Judy. "And maybe ask the guys what they think."

Bev frowned. There was only one guy she wanted to ask, and she was scared of what he might say. If he told her to play with the girls, did it mean he was eager to be rid of her? On the other hand, if he wanted her to stay and play with the guys, was he being selfish and short-sighted? Either way, the fact still remained: she had to play to win.

And winning would only make it harder.

5

If I Were a Rich Man

Twig had known of Reginald Fairview long before 1955. Most folks around town knew about the Fairview family and their prince of a son who was to inherit the Fairview family shipping and shoe manufacturing dynasty. Twig's high school football team would play Reggie's private school team about twice a year. Both had been quarterbacks, both talented on the field, both popular off the field, but Reggie had had all the other advantages Twig didn't, especially a proper upbringing by a family of means. Twig had never hated him for it, but he hadn't loved him for it either.

So when Marion Boggs and Reginald Fairview's engagement had been announced in all the papers, Twig had been skeptical. May Boggs, in his view, was a plain girl with a lower middle class background, like his own. Apart from being obviously book smart, the most she had going for her, as far as Twig had been concerned, was that she was Rowena Nolan's best friend. Twig had wondered why Fairview hadn't chosen Row. He had been relieved, of course, but he would have understood it. The Nolan family had some local fame (though for tragic reasons, but at least it was patriotic that all three of Row's brothers had been lost in World War II) and Mr. Nolan's family had amassed a modest fortune over several generations. And Row had been bright and easygoing and had that golden hair that absorbed and reflected all the light in any room she was in.

Maybe it was unethical—was there another word not so harsh? Twig couldn't think of one—when he had seen the watch that Row had brought in to the shop and known it was the same one May had brought in ten years earlier. Maybe it was unethical that he had gotten in touch with Reginald Fairview to ask about the watch and speculate with him about what it did. Maybe it was unethical to have inserted his agenda right in the middle of what could have been America's greatest love story, Prince Fairview and Pauper Boggs. And if it was unethical, he was paying his dues now. Trapped in a life that he hadn't chosen. Alone and aging, Row just out of his reach, while Mr. and Mrs. Fairview lived happily ever after—these had never been part of his plan.

May Boggs got a taste of what her best friend, Row, must have felt like mourning the loss of her family members. Lately, every big or small thing May did or experienced, she wondered what Emily Jackson would think, feeling her absence keenly. May pictured her laughing or crying or encouraging or scolding, depending on the situation. She secretly wondered what was worse: knowing that

someone you love is gone for good, or hoping they were coming back but never knowing. May, of course, wouldn't dream of asking Row's take on this, even though of the two of them, Row was in the position to know the answer.

So when May started her freshman year in college to get a secondary education so she could teach like her dad did, May knew that Em would be proud. May even wrote letters that she never sent, not having a forwarding address. For the first ten years after Em was gone, May replaced writing entries in her diary with writing letters to Emily. The letters stopped right around the time May got married to Reggie.

Dear Em,   Oct. 10, 1948

As always, I start with an apology. I'm sorry that I drove you away. I can hear you now denying it, but it was the watch that started it all . . . my watch. It was the watch that threw us back in time, that caused us to find out the truth about your family. I was so naive, thinking if you had the answers you could be happy. Now I truly understand the saying "ignorance is bliss."

I know other things that are bliss, too, though. The opposite of ignorance: knowledge. For every painful moment, life surprises me with an equal or greater reward—a revelation or a simple happiness. The adventure we had together was only the beginning.

sweet Emily. Because as I've said before, I'm sorry about another thing. I'm sorry I didn't tell you that I still had the watch. We could have gone back to 1864—if I could have figured it out—and I know how you wanted to check on the safe passage of Gin, Eliza, and baby Noah. I've become quite the liar, I confess. Mother thinks the watch is gone, just like you thought it was. But I continue to "come and go" without missing a day from home!

In my first week in college, I feel like I'm seeing my life in a new light. I have something to give, Em. I can hear your voice now: "I told you so, Marion Boggs!" It makes me smile. But sometimes we need to see ourselves through our friends' eyes. That's what I wish for you wherever you are. I wish you could have seen yourself through my and Row's eyes.

Of course, my mother is beside herself with de-spair with me in school. Since I'm 18 and have never had a steady, she thinks I'm already an old maid. Her only hope is that I'll go to college for a teaching degree but leave early with an M.R.S. degree. Meanwhile, I'm missing both you and Row since she left to travel and escape her stepmother. Things have not improved there, sadly. See how Row needs you? We both do.

Em, we do love you so and hope you'll come home to St. Louis soon or at least drop us a note. Wherever you are, I pray you are happy, safe, and healthy.

Always,

Marion G. Boggs

Dearest Em,   March 9, 1952

Happy birthday! I hope you are not a figment of my imagination. I wish I could hold you and grasp you and wish you a merry day in person.

I also wish I could see the look on your face when I tell you my good news. You already know I'm graduating in just a few months, but I've been offered a teaching job and you'll never guess where . . . at good old Roosevelt! I will start in the fall. Since Row has moved back to town, I will be living in the apartment recently built over the Nolans' garage. (Mother is fit to be tied. She doesn't want me to be an old maid, yet she wants me to live at home forever.

I haven't the foggiest what trouble she imagines I could get into, but if she only knew the places—times—I've gone right under her nose.)

And that's not all. I may not be getting my M.R.S. degree, but I did meet someone. He's as close to a prince as I could ever find. Even Mother would approve of him. Now, whether or not he knows my name is another thing, but I know he's not a figment of my imagination . . . and he's in the same dimension, so that's a promising start!

More details as they come . . . .

Always,

Marion G. Boggs

Reggie didn't know what to make of the letters. Already, Marion was like no other girl he knew, and certainly like no other he'd dated. There was a softness to her where other girls were brash, an intelligence and wisdom where other girls tried to be all sparks and laughs. And now he wondered at this quirky side of her. Were these pages of a manuscript she was writing? Certainly this Emily person could not have been real—or living; otherwise, why had Marion never sent the letters? He wanted to read more, assuming the "prince" referenced in the two-year-old letter was him, but he heard Marion finishing up in the restroom. Without thinking, he shoved the two letters in his sport coat and pushed the box containing many other pages back under the chair. His heart pounding, he didn't know how he could explain being caught snooping.

Marion emerged from the small bathroom, smoothing her skirt and wearing freshly applied lipstick. He was grateful for that split second of time while she looked down as he was able to regain his composure.

"Darling, you look perfect," he said in all sincerity.

She blushed, pushed her glasses up. "I hope this is appropriate for an evening at the theater." She gestured at her conservative, simple black dress with red piping trim.

"The Fabulous Fox theater can't compete with my magnificent Marion. Shall we?" Reggie held his arm out.

Reggie held his breath as she took his elbow and reached for her gloves next to the chair with her other hand. She glanced down, pausing ever so briefly at the sight of her misplaced inlaid box, at a slight angle under the chair. Reggie exhaled slowly as she seemed to dismiss whatever thought had occurred to her.

They enjoyed a lovely evening out; but Reggie found himself distracted when he looked at May. Was she a clever and creative woman, or was there something more disquieting about this person whom he had thought was so simple and transparent?

Two dates later, May told Reggie about a friend she and Row used to know named Emily who had left town years ago, never to be seen or heard from again. May said she wished Emily and Reggie could meet.

Reggie's mouth went dry involuntarily and he wondered just who Marion Boggs really was.

6

Take Me out to the Ballgame

Getting ready to warm up for the big game, Bev was alone in the girls' locker room, or so she thought.

"Have a good game tonight, Bev." Carla DiFrancisco's voice echoed off the metal lockers surrounding Bev.

Bev jumped, startled that she wasn't alone, but hid her surprise by leaning down to tie her cleats. "Thanks."

With Carla were two more of Bev's former—or soon to be again?—teammates. All Diane Dunkelman groupies. Diane was conspicuously absent, which was just fine with Bev. But Bev was suspicious anyway. She grabbed her bat, glove, and cap as quickly as possible and headed outside. The three trailed her.

"Hey, I hope you'll play with us tomorrow," Carla said and the others nodded.

"Thanks for the vote of confidence. We'll see." Bev wasn't just pretending to be noncommittal.

As she walked through the door into the muggy early evening, Carla said, "Now that Diane's off the team, we thought you'd love to play softball again."

Bev didn't reply and Lacy Garritson said, "We'll *all* love playing softball again," and the three of them laughed. Bev stopped and they almost ran into her.

"Watch what you say."

"What's your deal?" Carla sneered. "We thought you couldn't stand Diane."

"It's not about me, it's you. I thought you were her friends. And besides, isn't she your team captain? Show some respect."

"She *was*," Carla corrected.

Conrad, Bob, and Duncan Marsalis emerged from the boys' locker room next door. "Anyway, hope you'll consider playing with us," Carla said. The others called good luck to the guys and sauntered off.

"That did not just happen. Did I hear you stick up for Diane Dunkelman?" Bob goaded his sister.

"I didn't stick up for her. I just can't believe they call her a friend and talk about her like that."

"Well she is kind of a—" Marsalis trailed off as Bob punched him in the arm. Marsalis chuckled. "Sorry, man."

"She wouldn't exactly do the same for you," Conrad said.

"Oh, I know," Bev sighed. "It's just . . . I hate drama. I don't want any part of it."

Conrad smiled at that. Bob and Duncan trotted to the field, intermittently punching each other for fun.

"Can I ask you something?" Conrad said. Bev tried to make her "Sure" sound casual and he continued. "Why are people so ready to create drama?"

Without thinking too hard about it, she heard herself say, "Remember, Marshall, we have an outlet. We get to swing a bat, run fast, and play hard. Not everybody gets to do that. We create drama, we just do it differently."

He laughed, nodding, but he didn't seem as easygoing as usual. Bev longed to ask him what he thought of her playing in the girls' tournament tomorrow, but she didn't trust herself to talk about it and was concerned about his response. "What makes you ask?" she said, to keep herself from mentioning the tournament.

Conrad paused. "There's this woman. I love her—"

"Oh."

"—I mean, I'm *supposed* to love her. I *should* love her . . . but everything with her is a crisis. It drives me crazy. It should mean a lot to me that she's in town for my games—"

"Mm-hmm."

"—but really, I just want to play without any distractions, you know? Do you think that makes me a jerk? Be honest, Jenkins."

YES! Bev wanted to scream, but she understood. The part about distractions, anyway. "Of course that doesn't make you a jerk. It's not about who's in the stands tonight. It's about us." Bev felt herself flush and turned her head, fussing with her baseball cap. "It's about the team, I mean. Don't let her get to you."

"Thanks, G." Conrad winked at her and took off to jog the rest of the way to the field where Coach Riggins was rounding the team up for some baserunning drills.

Bev picked up the pace, too. The heat that she hadn't noticed before now felt suffocating and oppressive. Why couldn't she have been the girl her 1950s mother wanted her to be? Uninterested in sports, getting ready at home—putting a dress on to come to watch the game. And uninterested in a black guy. Life might be simpler if she were *that* girl.

Mary knew for certain that in 1955, Mom and Nana never would have let her ride in a car with a boy until she was at least sixteen. But now on her way out the door, she simply yelled out, "I'm going to the game with James and the girls," and Nana yelled back, "Call if you're going to be late." Mary couldn't decide if she liked that or not. Of course, it was swell to have the freedom to hang out with James, but she couldn't figure out why her mom was so paranoid about some things and unconcerned by others.

James made stops at Judy's, Maxine's, and Ann's after picking up Mary, and they filled his car with chatter and excitement for the game and wagering on whether Bev would play with the boys or girls the next day. Mary really wanted to talk about the watch and Mrs. F, but held off—she didn't want to come across as obsessed since no one else was talking about it.

Though they arrived at school with plenty of time before the game, the stands creaked and groaned with the weight of a growing crowd. Fortunately, Gary Jenkins, sitting with his parents and older brother, Jerry, had saved some seats and waved to James.

"Gary's sweet on you," whispered Judy to Ann, giggling.

"Oh, hush," Ann said, straightening her hat.

"You should go steady. Oh! Marry him and we'll be sister-in-laws!"

"*Sisters-in-law*," Mary corrected, then stifled a snicker.

"You're not helping," muttered Ann.

But when they made their way to the Jenkins and Gary said, "Ann, sit here," no one could deny that Ann had an admirer, not even Ann.

As the team warmed up on the field, Gary tried to banter with Ann, but she barely heard him. She thought of the latest email she'd gotten from her cousin Irina in Belgrade. Ann had been piecing together months of emails from Irina and studying the recent history of the former Yugoslavia. Her parents had left the Yugoslavian capital, Belgrade, in 1937, and things had deteriorated more than they could have imagined when the Nazis had taken over in the 1940s, "cleaning out" the Jewish population.

Ann was horrified to be learning that the wars in the 1990s hadn't been any better. Once again, the Jewish population, still diminished from World War II, had suffered even though they weren't specifically targeted; there was a whole new round of ethnic "cleansing" under and several wars in the region, resulting in millions of people displaced.

"What kind of music do you like?"

"I'm sorry, what?" Ann came to herself.

"I was just asking about music. But we don't have to talk." Gary seemed embarrassed that he was being ignored and Ann felt a twinge of guilt for being discourteous.

"I'm sorry, I guess I have a lot on my mind."

Gary seemed to see this as an opportunity. He perked up. "Like what?"

Ann didn't want to be rude, but she didn't know this boy and wasn't sure if she was in the position to be getting to know *any* boy. Her past and future both felt precarious. Sitting next to her,

Judy radiated positive energy like a visible wave of cheer. Some-times her perkiness was exhausting just to behold. Ann could appreciate, however, Judy's ability to make herself at home any-where . . . even fifty-five years into the future.

Taking Judy's lead, Ann tried to relax and conversed with Gary, starting with Irina and Belgrade, choosing to omit the other things on her mind: time travel, broken watches, and Mrs. F. "I suppose I'm worried about my cousin. She's a pen pal; I've never actually met her, but we're very close. She lives in Yugo— she lives in *Belgrade*—and I'm worried things aren't stable there for her."

"I *thought* I heard your family was from Belgrade!"

Ann furrowed her brows. Why did this seem so exciting to Gary? "My parents are, yes. But they—uh, my family—fled before World War II. We're Jewish, so we wouldn't have fared well."

"I had no idea you were Jewish."

Ann sat up a little straighter. This would be the test. Would Gary continue to fall all over himself for a Jewish girl? "Oh, yes; we used to be Orthodox. Before . . . well, times change, I guess. But I'm Jewish."

"I think that is so interesting."

Ann couldn't help but laugh now. "Which part?"

"All of it. I can't believe I didn't know you're Jewish. That's cool."

Judy, clearly eavesdropping, was beaming, but looking away from Ann. Ann couldn't help but be irritated by both Gary and Judy. *That's cool.* As if she needed his approval to be Jewish! In 1955, he certainly wouldn't have known she was Jewish because his mother asked Ann's mom, then the Jenkins' maid, to prepare the Christmas ham every year. Ann didn't know who irritated her more in that scenario: Mrs. Jenkins for not picking up on the fact that Katarina was Jewish and therefore didn't eat or prepare pork, or Ann's own mother for not standing up for her beliefs. Ann could see now why her parents were slacking in their observance. Maybe their religious zeal had been superficial all along.

"You know I'm doing an AP World History paper for Mrs. Fairview on the Balkans?" Gary said.

Now it was Ann's turn to be intrigued. "Really? That must be interesting. What are you learning?" Suddenly she was all ears.

The team cleared the field a few minutes before the start of the game. Bev hadn't stopped thinking about the girl Conrad loved. Fortunately for the Panthers, it had gotten her fired up and focused. Unfortunately for Bev, her insides felt raw.

In the dugout, Conrad sidled up to her, leaning against the railing and chewing gum. Bev wondered if she were going kooky.

"Hey, did you hear scouts are coming to the girls' softball game tomorrow?" she said casually. "They're putting together a national team."

"Yeah, I did hear. Bummer for you, huh? Too bad you'll be going to State with us." He winked at her, but she felt defiant.

"No, I won't. I'm going to play for the scouts."

"What?" Conrad straightened up. "Classy move, Jenkins. We make you one of the team and you abandon us when something better comes along. Nice."

"It's not like that," Bev said, berating herself for breaking her promise to keep her big trap shut.

"It's *just* like that, Beverly." Hearing him say her full first name smarted. "You're just like her."

"Who?"

"My mother," he said, exasperated. "I just told you about her!" Conrad shook his head and moved to the back of the dugout, mumbling, "She's going to play for the girls tomorrow."

The other players grumbled in protest, including Bob. "Are you kidding me? You get Diane kicked off the softball team so you can move in?"

"Of course not, Bob!"

Coach interceded. "OK, team. We need to focus on one thing and one thing only: winning this game. I don't want to hear anyone talking about tomorrow—*any* games tomorrow. There's only one. This one, right now." But he punctuated his speech by tossing Bev a dirty look.

Bev had to put aside Conrad's words: *My mother*. The woman he "should love" who was in town for his games. She had to put aside how awful she felt; worse than when she thought Conrad had a girl. Conrad had opened up to her and she had used it against him. There was nothing she could possibly say; there was only one thing to do and that was block it all out for now and play the best game of her life.

"I'm not playing for the girls tomorrow, Coach," Bev said, her voice sounding high and thin from desperation.

"No talk about tomorrow, Jenkins. What did I just say? There's only one game."

"Sorry, Coach." Bev tried to regather the energy she had been feeling. It was time to pitch.

The Panthers jogged onto the field, their fans jumping and cheering. But as their opponents prepared to bat and gathered at the railing of the visitors' dugout, the crowd calmed. Bev distantly wondered why, but threw some pitches to Marsalis. He seemed distracted by what the crowd was responding to. So Bev threw her hardest four-seam fastball to wake him up. He teetered back on his heels and Bev felt justified until the batter approached the box.

The Vikings had all slicked their lips with bright red, glossy lipstick. Their fans laughed and jeered and the Panthers fans murmured uncomfortably. At first Bev didn't get that they were making fun of her. What a dumb joke; she didn't even wear lipstick. But they were clearly making the point that they weren't intimidated by a girl.

Bev cocked her head at Marsalis. *Do you believe this?*

He smirked back. She liked his smirk. It meant he knew what was coming and the Vikings didn't. She nodded and grinned.

So, she'd get to play with the "girls" after all. She hoped their skills on the field were as lacking as their sense of humor.

"Let's do it, Jenkins," and "Smoke 'em, Bev," were heard around the diamond as her team rooted for her.

And with that, she hurled her first strike of the game at Marsalis's waiting glove.

7

For Future Reference

Row told May she was leaving to escape her parents—specifically her stepmother. But that was only partially true. Row could have taken up residence in the apartment over the garage and lived on her own terms, but she chose to travel instead. As was expected, her stepmother Gladys was scandalized at the notion of a woman traveling alone. But as he was in the habit of doing because he felt sorry for her, Mr. Nolan let Row have the final say. He knew she could take care of herself. But more than that, he'd lost the will to fight. This, ironically, was one of the reasons Row had to leave.

The other reason—and maybe even the bigger one—was May. After Em was gone, Row noticed funny things about May. A flush in her cheek, an air of excitement. Row confronted her, asking if May had "traveled" again. At first May wouldn't admit it, and then once when May was sleeping over, she and Row woke up in 1898. It was then that May confessed she'd had the watch back since soon after they'd returned from the Civil War.

Row hadn't had time to be angry; they were on their way to an 1898 St. Louis Browns vs. Chicago Orphans game. Row did have fun, but the time traveling had a different effect on her than it did on May. May was invigorated and inspired. Row grew weary and burdened. There had been enough unexpected change and "surprise" in Row's life to last a lifetime. She longed to feel settled again.

That's why the traveling she'd planned after high school ended after just a month, in Chicago. Row moved in with her Aunt Tessa — one of her father's seven siblings — and Tessa's husband, Ralph, and their three children in their suburban greystone northwest of the city. Row wasn't interested in college like May was. Row didn't want to be a teacher, a secretary, or a nurse, which were the limited options she had as an educated female. Instead, she started playing piano again and helping with her cousins to bide her time until she knew what she did want.

When she mentioned in passing to Uncle Ralph that she went to high school with the second string quarterback for the Los Angeles Rams, who'd been drafted before he finished college, football fan Ralph snatched up tickets for the whole family, spending most of his paycheck when the Rams came to play the Chicago Bears. Row never did see Twigler play because the Bears beat the Rams handily 24-0 and he stayed on the sidelines. She knew Uncle Ralph was hoping for an introduction after the game, but Row feigned illness and asked to go home. She didn't necessarily fault Twig for anything, she just didn't know if she could handle it if his eyes lit up when he saw her. For all she knew, he'd be married—most of their high school friends were.

After helping Aunt Tessa prepare dinner, Row excused herself to the guest room to lie down. Really, it was to just be by herself for a few moments. A knock came at her door.

Aunt Tessa and Uncle Ralph both crowded the doorway, excited.

"You have a gentleman caller!" gushed Aunt Tessa, a stocky, short, warm woman who looked especially short next to tall, skinny Uncle Ralph. Having never seen Row do anything remotely social in the year since she'd arrived, Tessa was thrilled by the prospect of a gentleman caller.

"I believe it's the boy who plays football!" Uncle Ralph said, equally enthused.

Row roused herself and began fussing with her hair. She suddenly felt nervous, but she wasn't sure why. Maybe it was the way her aunt and uncle looked at her with stars in their eyes.

"Well, we'd better not leave him with the kids too long," Row laughed, picturing how instantly Twig would become a jungle gym.

When Row emerged into the parlor, sure enough, two kids were literally hanging off of Tommy Twigler. He was using them as weights, pulling his arms up and down in curls.

"Michael! Lawrence!" Row reprimanded the boys since their parents were too starstruck to say anything. Their little sister Sylvia sat primly on the coffee table, watching with great interest.

"Hello, Rowena," Twig said. He leaned over to the coffee table where a bouquet of flowers lay on its side and offered it to her. She was not expecting the polished gentleman in front of her. As she accepted the flowers with a thank you, suddenly, her life passed before her eyes and she could see Tom Twigler as a father with a house full of kids—her house, her kids. It almost knocked her off her feet. She sucked her breath in and buried the image as deeply and as forcefully as she could.

"Tommy, how'd you find me?"

"Petey's working for his uncle at Jenkins Hardware. He said you'd moved to Chicago. You know how they are at the hardware store, everyone sharing news."

"Don't you mean gossip?"

Twig laughed. The kids now sat at Twig's feet staring up at him while their parents hovered behind Row.

The house was modest, especially compared to how and where Row had grown up, but the warm glow of home radiated from every lovingly cleaned surface. "Please come in. Can we get you some coffee or hot cocoa?"

Twig's expensive wool overcoat and hat were flecked with droplets of water that had been snowflakes before he'd come inside. Finally, Aunt Tessa found her bearings and sprang into action. She took the flowers from Row, shoved Ralph to take Twig's things, and hustled into the kitchen to put a pot of hot water on. The kitchen table was still full of plates as Twig had interrupted dinner.

"Your uncle also left word with the team manager that you were here and he supplied an address," Twig continued.

Row shot Uncle Ralph a dirty look, but he avoided her glare, taking Twig's coat to the coat tree at the bottom of the stairs. Twig noticed the dinner dishes on the table in the next room and apologized for interrupting, asking if he could take Row out for a cup of coffee. Row and the other Nolans all quickly declined—for different reasons—and Aunt Tessa brought in hot drinks and Twig's flowers displayed in a lustreware vase.

After several minutes of small talk, introductions, and Twig's corny jokes (which everyone but Row loved), Tessa announced it was the kids' bedtime. They protested that they hadn't finished dinner and weren't tired anyway, but Uncle Ralph cleared them out of the living room and excused himself as well.

Row was chagrined. Would Twig think it had been her idea to invite him here? The whole reason she was in Chicago was to escape St. Louis and everyone there. Row swallowed the last of her hot chocolate and didn't refill it, hoping Twig would take the hint. He had barely touched his coffee. Just as she'd feared, he'd settled himself comfortably into the sofa, draping one arm over the back of it as if the surroundings were familiar and he was perfectly at home.

"What do you fill your time with, Row?" Tommy asked conversationally.

Row was intentionally vague. "This and that. Helping Aunt Tessa with those little monsters; garden club; piano." She wished she could either ask him why he was really here or usher him to the door. Actually, both would have been ideal.

Instead, she courteously asked after him and what it was like living in Los Angeles. He told her about the lovely weather year round and funny stories about his teammates and the pranks they played on each other. While he spoke, Row thought of ways to politely get him out. She scolded herself for not saying she had a fella when Twig had asked what she did with her time.

"I might get traded to Chicago," Twig admitted suddenly.

"I thought you just said you loved California," Row said.

"Well, I do. But there's no one there for me. Here . . . ." Twig let his sentence dangle as Row mentally cut up the image of a family that had presented itself in her head earlier. Then she flushed the tiny pieces down an imaginary toilet.

"That's a shame because I'm moving myself."

"Oh?" Twig's face fell and Row's sympathy sparked for a second. "Where are you moving to?"

"Back to St. Louis," Row said spontaneously. St. Louis didn't have a football team.

"Row, to be honest, I—"

"Twig, it was my uncle's idea to give you this address. Not mine." Row spoke in no uncertain terms, but she couldn't look at him.

"I see." Twig seemed less confident now.

"I do thank you for stopping by. It's always nice to see an old friend." Row stood.

Twig remained seated, but looked deflated, as if he were a pillow on the davenport that desperately needed fluffing. "Was it something I said or did?"

The spark of sympathy ignited again and Row sat back down. "You didn't do anything. I am just not available." She almost added "ever," but her tone had enough finality in it to be clear. She wanted to squelch the man's dreams, but not the man himself.

Now Twig stood up and swiftly made his way to retrieve his coat and hat. He paused at the door.

"You deserve to be happy, Rowena Nolan." Twig spoke so quietly, she could barely hear him.

"Thank you, Tommy. So do you. That's why I'm asking you to leave."

Aunt Tessa crept in when she heard the front door latch. By the look on Row's face, she must have surmised they wouldn't be seeing Tommy Twigler again.

"But he reminds me of your brother Wally so; star football player, that goofy sense of humor . . . " Tessa said, urging Row to reconsider.

"I know, Aunt Tess."

Then Aunt Tessa saw, when no one else did, why Row had to let Twig go. Instead of being reminded of Wally Jr, Row was reminded that Wally Jr was gone. Along with Kell, Orvan, and her mother. She had even lost Finigan, her beloved dog. Friends and family could *cajole and encourage Row to get over her losses; and Row could tell herself a million times a day that her fear of loss was irrational, or that the tragedies she'd survived would never be repeated, but she kept coming back to this one fact: you can't lose something that you don't have in the first place. And she had made a note of that for future reference.*

Row and May stood practically under the bleachers in the one spot where they could see the game but not be seen.

"I don't know how I let you talk me into this," Row sighed.

"Talk you into this? I'm the one hiding under the bleachers with you because you 'didn't want to be seen.' I just thought you'd like to see Bev play. It's very inspiring."

"She couldn't do this in 1955, could she?" Row said.

May beamed. "No, she couldn't have."

Row glanced around her. No matter how many years had passed, it still felt strange to be on her old high school campus. Familiar feelings surged, filling her up and clogging her windpipe. Had it been this hard to breathe when she had attended school here?

"Looking for Twig? Is that who you're avoiding?" May asked. She said it playfully, but was only half teasing.

"Are you trying to match-make after all these years? It didn't work the first time and it certainly won't work now."

"Look! She struck him out!" May jumped and pointed at the field through the shoes, legs, and plastic cups decorating the stands in front of them.

Row clapped along with May, proud of Bev. At least that poor boy who had just struck out knew it was only a game. For some, it was life.

8

Win Some, Lose Some

Cheering for Bev and the Panthers was loosening Ann up. Maybe getting some attention from Gary wasn't such a terrible thing. She could always use another friend, right?

Gary continued to be fascinated with Ann's family's background in Yugoslavia, even though her knowledge of the region was mostly pre-World War II. He asked questions in between pitches and innings. Just when she was allowing herself to enjoy his company, he said, "Hey, would you mind if I emailed your cousin Irina? I'd love to hear from her firsthand what it's like living in Belgrade now."

"I don't think she'd mind," Ann answered, deftly evading his question as to whether she herself would mind.

"Awesome, Ann; thanks!"

She gave him Irina's email address and turned her attention to the game, where, she admonished herself, it should have been all along.

Bev was on a streak—three up, three down for the first three innings. Her pitching was perfect, but her hitting didn't follow suit. In fact, none of the Panthers were able to hit off of Bruce Miller, the big shot pitcher who'd taken the Vikings to State last year. His scarlet-stained lips had faded to their normal color, but his eyes had grown more steely and determined. Bev vowed to get a home run off of him if it was the last thing she did. Of course, Coach just wanted any of them to get on base; but Bev had bigger plans.

She tried to ignore the fact that though her team cheered her on, there was a cool reserve that reminded her of her first game with them, when they didn't know what to make of her. Besides being miffed at her, Conrad wasn't acting himself. He continually glanced into the stands. In the second inning, he'd let the shortstop snatch a ball out of the air that normally he would have dived for and come up with heroically. Fortunately, the ball was caught and they got out of the inning, but Bev could tell Conrad was preoccupied.

In the dugout, Conrad sat by himself, mopped the sweat off his face, and emptied a water bottle in practically one swallow. Bev approached stealthily, sitting near, but choosing carefully when to speak.

"Where is she?" she finally asked.

Conrad gestured toward the stands.

Bev asked him to point out his mom and he did.

"Well, Marshall, it's no use pretending she's not there, or pretending certain things aren't happening that are. But remember what I said? We all need an outlet. And this is yours. So take advantage. Don't do it for her . . . and for goodness' sake, don't *not* do it for her. Do it for you. And for us . . . for your team."

"You're right, Jenkins."

Bev was flooded with sweet relief to hear his normal tone of voice and to be called *Jenkins* again instead of *BEV-ER-LY*.

"If you need a little help, you can always wear some of my lipstick." She grinned.

He shoved her playfully. "Yeah, for that stunt alone we need to send these guys packing."

Marsalis overheard. "Let's do that."

A ripple of life flowed through the dugout and those who were sitting, stood up. They all leaned into the railing and starting cheering for Ray Darby, who was at bat. Bob was on deck. As if a call had gone out, the crowd got back into it, too. The atmosphere instantly recharged. Bev relished it: the rhythm of baseball. Just when it felt like nothing was happening, a tiny spark could light the place up. As certain as she was of the sun coming up in the morning, that's how certain Bev was that moment that they were going to win the game.

After taking two balls, Darby hit a line drive past the shortstop and rounded first base. The crowd roared. Darby played it safe, staying on first base, and Bob stepped up and Bev grabbed her bat. She knew Bob and she knew he'd be in the zone, with Darby on base and the crowd in the game, adoring him and screaming his name. For a brief moment, Diane Dunkelman flitted across Bev's mind. Diane would have loved this, would have loving cheering Bob on. And, if she was anything like Bev—and in this case, Bev knew she was—she'd be savoring tonight even more as she thought about her own softball tournament tomorrow.

Annoyed that now of all times she'd be thinking about Dun-kelman, Bev pushed Diane out of her thought and focused on the game and her impending at-bat. She stepped into the on-deck circle and took a deep breath.

Bob swung at the first pitch and missed, but the Vikings' catcher missed, too, and while he scrambled for the ball, Darby took second base. The pitcher looked annoyed. He threw one of Bob's favorite pitches, a fastball, but Bob didn't fall for it; before it reached home plate it sank and shot by Bob's ankles.

Bev took the scene in. This was the moment before the game became theirs. The momentum was shifting. She observed the Vikings (the outfielders had moved back), the crowded stands. She spotted Maxine, Mary, Ann; Gary sat next to Ann and on his other side, their parents and her older brother, Larry. She wasn't even annoyed this time that Ann and Gary looked so cozy. She surveyed most of the softball team, yelling their lungs out, supporting their friends on the boys' team. Such a strange phenomenon, baseball. When she was pitching, batting, or fielding, it felt like an individual sport. But it was all played with a team and their energy, their confidence, and their love of the sport made it what it is. They buoyed her and made her better.

As she did every time she played ball, she recalled attending her first game with Pops. Not only had Stan Musial broken a record (five home runs), but Bev had reveled in the camaraderie between the fans in the stands, the lull between the moments of action, and the sounds of the crack of the bat and the organ bleating out carnival tunes. Baseball was a game of faith, Bev decided. She had learned in Sunday School that faith was seeing what was invisible and baseball was all about believing in what is possible, even when it might not seem likely. After all, a 70%

failure rate was considered successful. It was what you *couldn't* see that made baseball great.

Another of Miller's sinkers sailed across the plate, but Bob got enough of it to drop the ball between the outfielders and the infielders. Darby stayed where he was at second and Bob was safe at first.

Bev stepped up to bat. Her usual apprehension—that a pitcher would see she was a girl and go easy on her—nagged at her. More than anything, she wanted Miller to pitch his best stuff. She craved for him to be intimidated by her in a different way: because she was a better player, not because she was a novelty. She tapped the dirt out of her cleats with her bat, felt the reverberation ripple up her leg. She pulled the helmet down tighter over her pony tail.

The fans behind her wore their voices raw with shouts of anticipation and approval, but the noises she loved to hear at the ballpark faded as she took a warm-up swing. Behind her, the catcher made kissy sounds; Bev couldn't have been happier. It would be that much more enjoyable to send the Vikings home so they could go to State—

Was she going to State?

Or would she play with the girls?

—No. Her job right now was to crush the ball beyond recognition. Her job was to wipe the bored look off of Miller's face and bring Bob and Darby home.

Keep making those kissy sounds, Lediski, Bev thought. *That's the sound of you kissing this game goodbye.*

Miller wound up. The pitch came in. It was perfect . . . . It floated right in front of Bev, practically stopping so she could count the stitching . . . .

"Strike!"

The crowd exhaled in a moan.

From the dugout, her team shouted encouragement. "It's OK, Jenkins!" "Come on, Bev!" and one voice rose about the rest, "You got this, G!" In that moment, Bev saw herself, feet planted, arms fully extended in a satisfying ache, having smashed the ball past Miller, over the outfielders, beyond the fence. She saw the little kids running back toward the field saying, "We can't find it!" when they went to look for the ball. She saw herself rounding first while Darby trotted over home plate, rounding second while Bob scored as well, and gliding home. Then she saw the final score of the game: Panthers 3, Vikings 0.

And apart from the kids not being able to find the ball in the parking lot, that's exactly what happened.

9

This is Not a Date

The ringing in her ears would never go away; her whole life, there would be a high-pitched buzzing accompanying everything Bev heard. She didn't care; it was from the wild screaming of her team and the crowd after the last pitch. The Fifties Chix were flushed with pride for their friend and stormed the field with everyone else. Bev was sorry to turn down their invitation to go to the fifties diner, citing the need (and, of course, her desire) to celebrate with her team.

"Call us and tell us what you decide," Ann yelled. She would have whispered it, but Bev would have missed it completely and no one else could hear her anyway, even though she was shouting. Bev's mood appeared to have dimmed for a moment, but she assured Ann she'd let her know.

When the congratulations and accolades died down and the crowd that hollered them thinned out, Bev was sorry to have to go to the girls' locker room by herself to clean up. The guys tripped into their locker room together, still hooting and celebrating, shoving each other playfully. She consoled herself that she'd catch up with them at the burger joint where they'd all agreed to meet. Conrad had been sure she would be there and now she especially wouldn't miss it for the world.

Bev hoped none of the softball players who'd descended on the locker room before the game would catch up with her there after the game. She got her wish, but she also got something else she hadn't bargained for: Coach Rasmus was in her office and came out when she spotted Bev. After complimenting Bev's pitching and hitting, she said simply, "Well?"

Bev longed to be in the shower by herself, hearing the echo of the hot water splash off the cold tiles, steam rising up around her while she reviewed the game, moment by moment, berating herself for the missed plays and reveling in the strikes she threw and the home run she hit. And then she would allow herself to think about what she should do about playing for the boys or girls before the water turned cold and she had to come back to the real world.

"I—I haven't . . . decided yet," Bev stammered.

"It's a tough decision to make in light of that game," Coach allowed.

Bev appreciated Coach's acknowledgment, but that didn't help either. After a long stretch of silence, Coach sighed. "Give it a little more thought, Jenkins, and call me if you want to talk about it; but I need to know yes or no to the tournament by six a.m. tomorrow." She handed Bev a business card with her contact information on it.

"Thanks, Coach."

At last, Bev could jump in the shower. As the hot water slid over her shoulders, making her hair a dark brown slick against her skin, she began her ritual of analyzing the last game played. Before she got through admonishing herself for the less-than-perfect plays, however, she heard the sharp, high-pitched whistle of her brother Bob.

"Jenkins! Let's go! Put on your makeup already, I'm leaving for the pizza party!"

"Coming!" Bev hollered and then the heavy metal door slammed closed.

She hustled out of the shower, drying off and getting dressed in record time. She toweled her hair dry as best she could in the humid atmosphere and looked for the rubber band she had used to hold her hair in a pony tail. Not finding it, she tried to tie her hair in a knot, but thin and slippery as ever, even while damp, it didn't stay put.

She sighed and grabbed her duffle bag, cleats, and favorite bat and ran to catch up with Bob.

"Bev, you look like a girl," Marsalis said, noticing her loose hair from the front seat as Bev slid in the back of Bob's waiting car.

"So do you, Duncan," Bev shot back. Bob and Marsalis laughed.

As they left the school grounds, Bev asked Bob about his mention of going for pizza. "I thought we were getting burgers. Does Con—does Marshall know?"

Bob and Marsalis snorted knowingly. Bev chose to ignore it and was grateful they didn't pursue teasing her for being concerned about Conrad's whereabouts.

"I don't know, Bev. We didn't send out engraved invites, a few of us just decided to grab pizza instead."

Marsalis turned on a CD full blast and rolled down the window so the world could enjoy his choice music.

After a moment of driving, Bev hollered over the bass, "Can we just swing by the burger place to make sure Conrad isn't there?"

Bob rolled his eyes, but swung the car around. A few blocks later, he screeched to a stop and demanded that she hurry up. She dashed inside, searching the small restaurant and spotted Conrad sitting alone with a towering burger in front of him. Two things occurred to Bev as she took in the scene: one, that Conrad was eating at what in the 1950s would have been a "white" establishment in the "white" part of town, and yet no one seemed bothered by his presence; and two, that Conrad looked really nice all cleaned up and sitting in a restaurant.

"Bev?" He looked at her quizzically. "Where's everyone else?"

"I came to tell you we're meeting at a pizza place."

"You came here just to tell me that? Why didn't you just call or text?"

Bev refused to look embarrassed and by force of will, kept her blush to a minimum. "We couldn't celebrate without you. And I don't have your number."

"I already started eating." Conrad gestured to the two plates mounded with food and the vanilla milkshake. "I'll come join you all later."

Bob honked from the parking lot, but Bev hesitated.

". . . or you can hang out here till I'm done and we can go together," Conrad suggested. Bev was certain the floor fell out from beneath her or she levitated several inches; either way, she felt temporarily weightless.

"OK. I'll be right back." Bev went out to tell Bob and Marsalis that she and Conrad would join them later. Saying "Conrad and I" and "we" tasted as sweet as candy. As they raced off in Bob's car, smirks on their faces, Bev practically skipped back into the restaurant.

She settled into the bench across from him in the booth, trying to not smile like a dope. Conrad motioned for the waitress and asked Bev what she wanted to order. She stopped herself from saying that she would just get pizza later, determined to draw out this time alone with Conrad as long as possible. "Root beer float," she said. "And double cheese burger, please."

Conrad pushed a plate of French fries in her direction. "Have some," he offered. Then he looked at her, his head tilted. "Your hair. You look like a girl."

Bev recalled what a hit her "So do you" retort had been in a car, but opted to go another direction this time around. "I *am* a girl," she said instead.

When their server brought Bev her order, Bev studied her reaction; but the waitress seemed unconcerned that a black boy and a white girl were eating together. Bob and Gary sure didn't seem to have a problem with the idea that she liked Conrad. She wondered what her non-1955, present-day parents would think.

They chatted easily about the game, Bev comfortable with the topic and eager to relive their team's dazzling victory. But right before they finished clearing their plates, the conversation inevitably turned to the games the next day and whether Bev planned on being there. She had hoped that maybe sitting there with Conrad, spooning root beer-soaked ice cream into her mouth, she would feel impelled to play with the boys. But surprisingly, she didn't have the clarity she'd expected.

"Don't be sore at me," Bev said.

"Why would I be?" Conrad said, amused by her word choice.

"Because I don't know what I'm going to do. What would you do in my shoes, *honestly*?"

Conrad raised his eyebrows, considering. "You got me. I know what I think from my point of view, but not from yours."

"What's your point of view?"

"Hey, they've got video games here. Wanna play?" He gestured toward the back wall of the small diner, which was starting to fill up with the after-movie crowd.

Bev heard the word "games" and agreed. They wandered over and Conrad dumped a load of quarters into the upright machine, hit a few buttons, and then began blowing things up on screen. His whole body rocked as he pounded the controls. Bev found the explosions and beeping and electronic music irksome and wondered what Conrad enjoyed so much about it. When it was her turn, it didn't take long for the screen to explode and a sappy loser tune to emit from the machine.

"Ah, Bev, you gotta shoot to kill, see . . . . " Conrad was about to give her instructions when her eyes locked on a nearby pinball machine.

"Pinball!"

"You think you're any better at pinball?" Conrad said. His tone was doubtful.

Bev flashed him the smile she gave Marsalis right before she struck out a heavy hitter. Conrad took the challenge and moved to the pinball machine, loading it with quarters. This time Bev went first. She tucked her hair behind her ears (not that it did any good) and leaned into the glass-topped horizontal cabinet, hands on the flipper control buttons. The machine came to life, dinging and buzzing, flashing and blinking as she shot the steel ball into the targets and earned more steel balls.

Conrad laughed and hollered, pointing at her next target and encouraging her to keep going. Soon, a few people on their way to or from the restroom stopped out of curiosity to watch and the crowd grew. After Bev had won herself three free games, the crowd consisted of everyone in the restaurant except a young couple in a corner booth too obliviously in love to notice any one else. Like the crowd at the baseball game just an hour beforehand, this group cheered Bev on. Finally, the machine lit up and played a cacophony of tinny victory music, announcing Bev had earned the high score. Everyone, including their waitress and one of the cooks, let out a loud cheer as Conrad threw his arms around Bev and lifted her off the ground.

"Your girlfriend plays a mean pinball, son," laughed an older gentleman, heartily clapping Conrad on the back.

Bev was about to protest to allay any awkwardness Conrad might feel, but Conrad agreed, saying, "You should see her on the pitcher's mound!"

Bev beamed.

On the way home in Conrad's dad's car—the two of them having decided they'd missed the majority of the pizza party—Bev savored the warm glow that came from deep within and radiated all around her. This unfamiliar feeling of peace and exhilaration swept her up and rocked her like a gentle but forceful wave. She wondered, had she just had a date with Conrad Marshall? If so, it was better than she could have imagined.

"Conrad," she said, intentionally using his first name. "I think I decided who I'm playing for tomorrow."

Conrad smiled. "Yeah, I bet you have. So, what's it gonna be?"

"I'm playing the softball tournament. With the girls." Bev grinned, triumphant that she had made a decision that felt right.

Conrad, on the other hand, abandoned his smile for a frown. "Are you kidding me right now, Jenkins?" His using her last name stung a little.

"Well, no . . . I thought . . . ."

"You thought it would be cool if we had a fun night out as teammates—" there was that stinging sensation again "—and then you'd desert your team for your own selfish gain? Am I supposed to be cool with that?"

"It's not like that," Bev insisted.

"Then explain it, Miss Pinball Wizard."

"Put yourself in my shoes, Marshall," Bev said, adding his last name with an edge.

"I don't have the luxury of being in your shoes."

They'd pulled up in front of Bev's house without her having to give him directions. He stopped the car and stared ahead. A wall had gone up between them and Bev didn't know how to scale it. Conrad had already admitted that he wouldn't know what to do in her shoes, but he obviously had an opinion about what she should do. So, would it please him if she changed her mind and decided to go play with the boys tomorrow? But Ann and Judy had said to follow her heart and that's what she was doing. *Unless you counted being on Conrad Marshall's team as following your heart,* she sighed.

"Good night, Conrad. Thank you for a lovely evening."

"Night, Jenkins. Congrats on your big win. Or should I say, *wins.*"

Bev got out of the car and loped up the path to her front door. Before she'd even reached the first step, Conrad sped off. Bev whirled around. "You are so rude, Conrad Marshall!" Her scream echoed off the neighbors' houses and two dogs went into barking fits. Clutched was worse than losing a game, the biggest of the season and it made her blood boil.

She went in the front door and slammed it, satisfied when the whole wall shook and the family photo hanging on it went crooked.

10

Like I Really Care

DISTRICT CHAMPS, JUST LIKE I PREDICTED!! WHAT A SWEET GAME. STARTED SLOW, MY HEART WASN'T IN IT. BUT THE TEAM RALLIED, INCLUDING BEV JENKINS, WHO WAS PITCHING. HAVE I MENTIONED HER? JUST FLIPPED THROUGH MY JOURNAL; I GUESS NOT. THOUGHT I HAD. ANYWAYS . . . . HERE'S HER DEAL. SHE PITCHES LIKE HER LIFE DEPENDS ON IT; I WOULD NEVER SAY THIS TO HIS FACE, THOUGH HE PROBABLY KNOWS IT, BUT SHE PITCHES BETTER THAN HER BROTHER BOB. SHE FINDS OUT RIGHT BEFORE THE GAME THAT SHE CAN EITHER GO TO SEMIS AND STATE WITH US TOMORROW—

OR GO PLAY SOFTBALL WITH THE GIRLS WHERE THEY WILL HAVE SCOUTS PUTTING TOGETHER A NATIONAL TEAM! MUST BE NICE!

WE ENDED UP HAVING BURGERS TOGETHER AFTER THE GAME AND HAD A GREAT TIME PLAYING PINBALL AND I REALLY FELT LIKE WE WERE ON THE SAME TEAM. THEN SHE ANNOUNCED SHE'S GOING TO GO PLAY WITH THE GIRLS AND ACTED ALL SURPRISED THAT I'M NOT PSYCHED FOR HER. DID SHE WANT ME TO BEG HER TO PLAY WITH US? I'M NOT PLAYING THAT GAME, I'M NOT BUYING INTO THE DRAMA.

IT'S JUST ONE MORE DISAPPOINTMENT FOR CONRAD MARSHALL. AT LEAST I STAYED OUT WITH HER LONG ENOUGH TO AVOID SEEING MOM. SOME TRADE-OFF.

WISH ME LUCK TOMORROW.

PEACE OUT,

C.M.

❖   ❖   ❖

To: \<Irina Brajer\>
From: \<Gary Jenkins\>
Date: May 28, 11:14 pm
Subject: Favor for Ann's friend?

Hi Irina,

My name is Gary Jenkins and I'm a friend of your cousin (Ann). I hope it's okay that I'm emailing you (she gave me your address). I'm writing a history paper about the Balkans and Ann speaks so highly of you. She thought you might be able to help me sort out some of my facts.

I am mostly wondering about how the war in the 1990s affected your life then and how it's affecting your life now. (I'm sorry to hear about the loss of your mother. I know it must be a sensitive topic and if you don't want to respond to this email I understand.) I understand that Belgrade was the seat of riots against Milošević when he tried to steal the election in 1993. If you are a couple of years older than Ann, that must have been around the time you were born?

Please let me know if you're willing to do me this big favor; if not, no worries. But my paper is due on Monday, so it would be great to know either way.

Thanks,

Gary

Gary hit "send" and leaned away from the computer. He thought he heard a faint yelling outside and then Bev storming up the stairs.

As she stomped past his room, he rolled his chair toward his door. "Hey, great game tonight."

She glared at him. "What?"

"I said, great game . . . . What's going on with you?"

"Just when everything is perfect, it's not!"

"Would you care to elaborate—"

"I'm playing with the girls tomorrow and you can't talk me out of it and neither can anybody else. I've made up my mind!" She thundered off, slamming her bedroom door across the hall.

"Alrighty, I guess I won't try to talk you out of it," Gary muttered.

His computer dinged. New email:

From: <Irina Brajer>

To: <Gary Jenkins>

Sent: 29 May, 6:17 am

Subject: RE: Favor for Ann's friend?

Of course I'll answer your questions. I'm happy to help any friend of my cousin's. I'm so glad she's made a new friend to get her mind off the other boy.

Life is not easy here, depending on where you live. Some parts of the city go on as if nothing has ever happened. That's not true for Father and me, who are Jews and in the minority. It is my dream to move to New York City—where Ann and I will be roommates. Did she tell you?

Yes, the year I was born was a difficult year in beautiful Belgrade with the rise of civil war, but not as bad as the bombing by NATO on April 23, 1999 when I was six years old. I will forever remember this day, for this is the day my mother was taken from me. NATO bombed the Serbian television headquarters to "disrupt the communications network," as a report afterward mildly put it. That same report stated that the attack was "legally acceptable." I suppose that's the problem with war; attacks are legal or strategic or "acceptable," unless someone you love is killed. Then they are horrific.

My father will not leave Serbia. I cannot explain why except that he doesn't want to leave the last place my mother lived. He is holding out hope that Serbia will someday be what it once was, but one thing I have not told Ann because I do not want to worry her is that anti-Semitism is on the rise. For us, Serbia will never be what it once was. I am old enough to emigrate, I suppose, as many Jews have done (to the United States, Israel, or Hungary), but I cannot leave my father. It breaks my heart to imagine him living here alone. There is one Jewish synagogue remaining in all of Serbia and it is here in Belgrade.

I don't know if I've answered your questions. You may write me back and ask me anything.

Sincerely,

Irina

To: <Irina Brajer>

From: <Gary Jenkins>

Date: May 28, 11:20 pm

Subject: Re: RE: Favor for Ann's friend?

Hi Irina,

Thanks for the email back! I looked up the time difference; you're up early.

You said I could ask you anything . . . so here goes. What other boy was Ann's mind on?

Gary and Irina emailed back and forth until just before dawn in Gary's time zone. Irina had to sign off to wait tables at a café near her house. Gary was thrilled he'd found such a helpful resource: Irina knew a lot, and not just about Belgrade and the Balkans. She also knew a lot about her American cousin, Ann.

Bob rolled over and groaned. Why hadn't he turned his phone off? It wouldn't be a problem if he could fall asleep— once he crashed, nothing could wake him. But he was wide awake at midnight, still high from the big win, frustrated with his sister, and excited for tomorrow's games. He told himself to ignore the text, but he was awake anyway, so he retrieved his phone.

R u up. Great news!! Coach Raz just texted me & said I could play tomorrow in tournament. Guess they couldn't do it without me after all! ;) Congrats on your win 2nite <3

Bob sat up. That was strange. He wondered why would they decide to let Diane play after all that trouble she'd caused. And then he thought with a wicked smile how Bev would feel once she found out she'd have to play with Diane after all. That's what she got for leaving the boys' team high and dry. He felt a little guilty, but not much. *Bev* hadn't seemed to feel any guilt. He turned his phone off, rolled over and drifted off instantly.

"Coach? I'm sorry it's so late, but you said if I needed to talk . . . . Oh, this is Beverly Jenkins calling."

"I figured it was you when I saw your name on my caller ID. Of course it's not too late, this is why I get paid the big bucks."

"Really?"

"No, not really," Coach chuckled. She sounded sleepy and Bev felt bad. "You can call me anytime, but not because I get paid for it; because I care. So what's on your mind?"

Bev took a deep breath. "I want to play with the girls tomorrow."

"That's great! Do you feel good about that?"

"I do, but not everyone else does."

"That's to be expected. Thanks for letting me know—"

"There's more." Again, Bev inhaled and this time exhaled very slowly. "I think Diane Dunkelman should be able to play, too."

11

Lost & Found

Rowena hadn't meant to make a prediction about moving back to St. Louis in her conversation with Twig, but when her stepmother wrote about Wally Nolan Sr.'s health issues, within weeks, Row packed her belongings and headed home. On the train ride, she tried to rally, thinking of all the things she loved about St. Louis: her big old house, baseball games, Ted Drewes frozen custard, Forest Park in all seasons.

But getting off the train and seeing her dad and his replacement wife immediately reminded Row of what St. Louis—home—had come to mean to her: people who were gone. And not only her family, but Emily Jackson too. Even Marion Boggs, who was still living, but not present (by more than one definition!). Row and May wrote each other faithfully, and May's most recent letter announced that she had gotten a teaching job at their high school alma mater. May's other letters were full of details about her time travel adventures, and Row was reluctant to endorse May's adventures in case they drove her away for good like they had in Emily's case. But Row didn't have the heart to throw the letters out, and so they were tidily packed in a bundle in her steamer trunk.

The brisk February air that blasted Row's face when she descended the train steps at the Kirkwood depot smelled distinctly of St. Louis: coming rain, Mississippi mud, and heartbreak.

May came for dinner and Row was surprised to realize upon seeing May how much she had missed her. They pulled an all-nighter, whispering and giggling over hot cocoa. At first, there was no talk of time travel, no talk of disappointment or loss. They played catch-up and Row shared funny stories about her young cousins and their mischievous antics. May told Row about college life, including the dances and parties. And, most importantly, the Valentine's dance the week before where she had met a fellow named "Reginald Fairfield"—

"You mean, Reggie Fairview?" Row squealed.

"Yes, that sounds right."

"You know who he is, don't you? He's practically famous! We played him all the time in football in high school and he comes from a very wealthy family."

May's face fell. "Now that I think of it, he was surrounded by girls."

Row studied her friend: May's at times frantic enthusiasm had matured into a mellow confidence while she still maintained her sweetness and optimism. She was bright and insightful as well as book smart. She had an adventurous spirit and was loyal to a T. Reggie Fairview couldn't do any better than Marion Boggs and Row told her so.

"Did you talk to him at all?" Row asked.

"We even danced together! Of course, he danced with a lot of girls. But I don't think he came with a steady."

"Tommy Twigler came to see me. In Chicago."

"Twig? Well, how do you feel about him?"

Row fidgeted. She hadn't wanted to bring it up; they were having such fun talking about everything else. She avoided answering May's question. "He didn't exactly come to see me, he was playing in a professional football game—he plays for the Los Angeles Rams—"

May waved her hand impatiently; she knew all that. "What happened?"

"He didn't stay long; I asked him to leave."

"Oh." May seemed disappointed.

Row spent the next four minutes talking in circles about why things between Twig and her could never work out. May stayed quiet, but she noticed that not once did Row say she didn't like Twig. In high school, when Twig had wooed Row on her front porch, Row hadn't seemed to mind him and May had wondered if at the time, Row had held back because May had liked him.

"Will you do me a favor, Rowena Nolan?"

"Anything."

"Will you promise me you'll say yes if he asks you on another date?"

"He won't."

"If he does. . . . Promise me."

"I promise," Row sighed as the sun lit up the sky at dawn.

A year later, May was going steady with Reginald Fairview and Twig had stopped playing pro ball and had moved back to St. Louis. Row heard about Twig at Jenkins Hardware, where she'd gone to browse their seed selection and plan for her early spring plantings. Her dad was feeling better, and had been the day after she moved home, actually. So the nursing and companioning she'd expected to be doing at home was replaced with yard work—her favorite pastime—and piano. She had no plans to get married, didn't aspire to go to college, and found that not having plans for the future left the present rather empty. She'd always secretly wanted to be an aviatrix, but that seemed like a daunting undertaking besides being an outlandish dream.

So, as she was flipping through the marigold seed packets and overheard Mr. Jenkins—a big sports fan—tell her neighbor, Mr. Snyder, in the nuts and bolts aisle that Tommy Twigler had moved home, Row remembered her promise to May and she saw Twig in a new light. Also playing a role in that "new light" was how Row saw no future of her own emerging out of her aimless life, while May was being courted by Reggie like his life depended on it.

Sure enough, the next day, when Row was in the back garden building cold frames to house the seedlings she would be planting within the next couple of weeks, Tommy called on her. He walked around the back of house, Row's stepmom Gladys running after him in a tizzy, wailing, "She's not dressed to receive company!"

Twig laughed when he saw Row. In overalls and bundled in wool from the waist up, she looked like one of Santa's gardening gnomes, if there was such a thing. Her turquoise and red sweater and bright green hat were the only spots of color in a long, dreary February.

"Twig!" Row said with a little more delight than she'd meant to convey. She put out her hand to shake his and Twig laughed again, seeing her mittened hand wrapped around a hammer.

"Oh." Row snickered, laying aside the hammer.

"I daresay, young man—" Gladys puffed, catching up to him.

"It's OK, Gladys. Thank you," Row assured her. Gladys went back to the house, but had a scowl on her face as overcast as the gray day.

Tommy asked if he could help, to which Row said no; Row asked if he'd like some hot tea, to which he said no. So she kept working in an attempt to stay warm. They had a banal conversation which included a brief overview of Twig's career-ending injury (though Row couldn't see how it was career-ending; it sounded more like Twig had given up) and Row's plans for her garden. And then Twig cut to the chase and asked Row on a date for Saturday night. Row agreed, and it wasn't until she was putting rollers in her hair before bed that she realized Saturday was Valentine's Day.

On the day her dad had come to school to tell her about her mom's passing, before she'd left the classroom, Twig had given her a look of understanding pity. That was the day Row had decided no one would be taken from her again.

If only it had been in her power to keep such a promise.

When Twig looked back on that Valentine's date with Row, he couldn't figure out what had gone wrong. All of his high school buddies and football cronies had been getting married and starting families—some of them with little money, some with little smarts and some with no looks. Even those lacking all of the above were still walking down the aisle. Twig had saved up some money, was shrewd (if not smart), and had been told he was good-looking. So why had Row made it so difficult?

Was it the flowers he had brought her when he'd picked her up? Too pushy? Had he talked about himself too much? But when he'd asked her questions, she'd become more reserved and elusive. Halfway through dinner, Twig had felt the distance between them growing. He'd wanted to grab her hand, tell her how he felt, but he hadn't been able to find the words to say he knew what she'd been through, that he had lost his parents and family at a young age; that he wanted to make up for it and would spend his life making her smile. He'd make sure she had the biggest plot of land in town if she wanted to spend all day gardening. But when he'd opened his mouth, nothing had come out except for a snide remark or a joke. And . . . he'd noticed those were decidedly *not* making Row smile.

On the quiet ride home in his foster dad's old Ford, Twig had worked up the courage to tell Row what was on his mind . . . on their next date. But there had been no next date. At least, not for two more years until she'd come into the shop with that "broken" watch. Before then, there had only been hearing about her via town gossip, or seeing a picture in the paper of her standing next to Marion Boggs and her beau, Reginald Fairview, at some social event. He'd felt he should have been standing on the other side of Row, where there was always an empty space. No amount of physics, astrophysics, or electromagnetic technology could put him in the space next to her . . . or fill the empty space in his heart. And it wasn't for lack of trying. He'd jumped at the chance to change his focus; he'd moved to New York. But when the program had shut down there, he'd come home to St. Louis and certain emptiness.

Now Tommy was just old Twig, too old to make a life for anyone other than himself and stuck in the past in a most ironic way. All the work he had done to control time, control his destiny, and he was still helpless.

So when his doorbell rang early that Saturday morning with Mary Donovan, Maxine Marshall, Judy White, and Ann Branislav standing expectantly on his front stoop, he was as caught off guard as ever.

12

Teamwork / Dreamwork

Conrad Marshall took Beverly's hand, squeezed it, and looked at her as if really seeing her. His eyes were as warm and deep and steady as Bev had always imagined and now his expression was sincere.

"Jenkins, I never should have sped off last night. In fact, I'm skipping our games so I can come see you play."

Bev should have been overwhelmed, but she checked herself: she felt totally normal. Overcome with happiness, but otherwise normal. Conrad's hand, with hers still in it, swung down at his side and he turned and they walked down the hall together. No one noticed, except for Miss Boggs, who gave Bev a wink *through her cat-eye glasses,* standing in her classroom door. Bev liked that Conrad was wearing her letterman's jacket. Their sneakers squeaked in time with each other on the old linoleum school tiles and they laughed about it.

At the end of the hall, the school doors were propped open to reveal a blazingly bright day. Fresh air gushed toward them and they sped up. They didn't want to be late for the game. But when they emerged into the sunshine, the temperature dropped sharply and clouds rushed overhead. Everything was different: the towering, aged trees surrounding their old school were gone and in their place was a field of drooping saplings.

"They're dying!" Bev exclaimed.

Conrad dropped her hand and backed away. She turned to reach for him again, but he had vanished. Mrs. Jenkins in her 1950s hair, wardrobe, and ruffly, well-pressed apron bolted to Bev, grabbing her shoulders and shaking her sharply. "I saw you with him! I saw you! Never, ever, ever see him again, Beverly Jean Jenkins! I forbid it!"

"Conrad! Mother, no!" Bev cried out.

"It's for his own good!" Mrs. Jenkins insisted.

Bev sucked the whole room full of air into her lungs and sat up. The drowning sensation ceased instantly, but her heart hurt and her shoulders were still being grabbed.

"My word, sweetheart; you must have been dreaming!" Bev's mom looked alarmed.

Bev adjusted her eyes. Modern mom, loose hair, no makeup, still in her robe, and no smell of breakfast cooking. Bev's stomach clenched. Was she relieved or disappointed to wake up and still be in the future? Her hand was glowing with warmth, as if Conrad was still holding it. She felt her cheeks go pink under her mom's gaze.

"What did I say?"

"Something about Conrad's mother, I think."

"Oh." Bev pulled her knees up to her chest, and with it her blanket. Though the temperatures soared outside—even this early in the morning—her house was chilly. The air conditioning ran nonstop.

"Your brothers told me you decided to play with the girls today. Why didn't you tell me yourself?"

Bev scrutinized her mother, trying to decide if her mom was reprimanding her for not telling her, or honestly expecting Bev to confide in her. Bev shrugged. "Are you mad?"

"Of course not. I just know that can't have been easy for you. I know I haven't been around much because of work. I had thought that with you in high school now, it would be easier for me start the business with Kat, but it's taken me away from you more than I'd planned. I miss you."

Bev launched herself into her mother's arms and time stood still. It could have been 1946, her first day of school, when her mom held her tight. Bev hadn't wanted to admit that she had been scared; after all, her three big brothers had been going to school and they hadn't been frightened. She had wanted to be as tough and brave as they were. As her mother had embraced her then, she had said to Bev, "You don't have to be brave; you're a girl." The words had cut Bev to the quick, so she had burrowed herself deeper into the hug for comfort.

Now, she was just as ambivalent about her relationship with her mom, hesitant to confide in her in case her mother's response was more painful than the distance between them. She tested the waters. "What would you have told me if I had asked you about it?"

Bev's mom stroked Bev's hair and Bev felt her mom's chin gently bump the top of her head as she talked. "I would have asked you what you wanted. I would have reminded you that no matter what team you chose, you would be a boon to them and they would be fortunate to have you."

Bev pushed a little bit more. "What if I told you there's a boy on the boys' team that I like?"

Her mother chuckled. "That does complicate things. But we all have to learn that following your heart doesn't just mean following after a boy. You made a wise decision."

Bev pulled away from her mom, surprised. "Really?"

Mrs. Jenkins laughed. "Yes, really. Following your heart means doing what is best for you, putting yourself in the best position to make a meaningful contribution. Maybe the most meaningful contribution you can make is to be on a girls' national team."

Bev hugged her mom again, hiding the tears that had sprung to her eyes. "I miss you, too, Mom." Bev realized she didn't just miss her mom since Bev had woken up in the future; she had missed her mom her whole life.

Bev wanted to ask her mother what she thought of Conrad, but didn't want to ruin the moment. Plus, she remembered, she was still mad at him.

"Where did you get the apron?" Judy asked sleepily, yawning and reaching for a mug to pour herself some coffee.

Mary, abashed, looked down at her dainty, frilly, floral smock. "I brought it with me." She didn't need to say that she had made it.

After Bev's baseball game last night, Mary, Judy, Ann, and Maxine had gone to their new favorite hangout and then decided to have a sleepover; since Bev had declined the offer to join them for a soda, they had hoped she wouldn't mind if they had a slumber party without her. Plus, she had big games today, whomever she decided to play for. Mary realized how silly she must have seemed to Judy, throwing together things for an overnight at the last minute and including an apron. But Mary had known that she would be the one up early making breakfast, so she had wanted to come prepared.

Indeed, while her friends still dozed on the floor in the living room, she had roused herself and headed for the kitchen. She had found egg substitute, almond milk, and oatmeal. Not exactly her usual gourmet palate, but she did her best. She made a note to herself to ask James why there weren't normal foods like whole milk, sausage, bacon, flour, and sugar in the future. As far as she knew, they weren't being rationed. Then again, Judy's mom, Bitsy, never had been a whiz in the kitchen.

"Nothing for me, thanks," Judy said, pouring herself a cup of coffee.

Mary frowned. She had noticed last night that Judy hadn't had anything at the café except a glass of ice water with lemon. "Breakfast is the most important meal of the day," Mary said, stirring the oatmeal. "You—we," she amended, "are at a crucial growing stage and should be eating—"

Judy laughed and interrupted Mary. "OK, *mother*, thank you." (If only she would get a speech like that from her mom.) "Which do you think she'll choose? Boys or girls?" Judy reopened the discussion they'd had at least four times last night about Bev.

"Boys," voted Maxine on her way into the kitchen. She wore a scarf on her head and a large T-shirt from her sister's college. "Can I help?" she asked Mary.

Mary shook her head no and scooped out oatmeal into four bowls, despite Judy's protest. By the time Ann had joined a few minutes later, they were back on the topic of Bev's baseball vs. softball dilemma again. Maxine was the only one who was certain Bev would choose to play with the boys, but she refused to explain her reasoning to the others. She knew that Bev liked Conrad, but Maxine wasn't about to be the one to spill the beans about that.

"Bev better let us know soon so we can go watch her play," Ann worried, polishing off the rest of the oatmeal, even though she knew it wasn't kosher. She had given up observing and was now working on not feeling guilty about it.

As if on cue, the phone rang and Judy jumped up to answer it, her oatmeal and fried eggs both untouched. After answering, she gestured wildly that Bev was on the other line. She gave a thumbs-up sign to her friends and reported, "Girls' team!" but her smile quickly turned sour. She mumbled her best wishes and goodbyes and rejoined her friends at the table, looking distressed.

Her friends were excited Bev had chosen to play with the girls' team, and Maxine was particularly impressed, but they didn't understand Judy's response.

"She convinced Coach Rasmus to let Diane Dunkelman play."

Judy's friends stared at her in disbelief and the room fell silent as they pondered this strange news.

"Maybe Bev didn't want people to think she'd gotten Diane kicked off the team so Bev could be the star," Mary speculated.

"Bev isn't that cunning," Ann objected. "And I don't think she cares that much what people think."

"What about what Diane did to Maxine?" Judy said.

Maxine quickly jumped in. "I'm not worried about that. We'll just have to ask Bev when we see her." They had all learned to give each other a little credit and not jump to conclusions, so the others agreed with Maxine.

"In the meantime," Mary said, clearing the dishes, "we still have our work cut out for us. I volunteered us to do the retrospective for Mrs. F's retirement and we only have five more days."

The girls couldn't believe Mary had volunteered them for the project.

"It's an excuse to do some more digging and sleuthing. And it's an excuse to talk to Twig. Look, I found a picture of him in Mrs. F's yearbook." Mary put the dishes in the sink and retrieved the old yearbooks, which she had packed along with her apron.

Mary had bookmarked several pages and turned to the one with Twig and a group of kids cutting up. "How does he know about Mrs. F's watch?" Ann puzzled.

"That's what I'd like to know," Mary said.

"Hey, it says here he's with Peter Jenkins." Judy tapped the photo thoughtfully. "Do you think that's Bev's uncle?"

"Must be; he looks like Bob," replied Ann. *And Gary,* she added silently.

"Oh, yeah." Judy smiled.

Maxine looked at the others in the photo. "Who's this Emily Jackson?"

"We need to find that out, too. She was Miss Boggs's and Aunt Row's best friend, but I don't know what became of her," said Mary. Whether they found out anything useful or interesting, she almost didn't care. She was just tired of not having any answers at all.

"She looks familiar somehow," Maxine noted. "Why don't we just ask Mrs. F or Aunt Row about this Emily person?"

"It's supposed to be a surprise for Mrs. F and Aunt Row is clamming up. Now whenever James asks her questions, she gets real nervous," explained Mary.

"Well, where do we start, then?" Judy asked, gulping down the rest of her coffee.

"I think a field trip to Mr. Twigler's house on our way to Bev's games is in order."

The other girls agreed with Mary and helped her clean up the rest of the dishes. Before Bitsy was awake, they were out the door to Twig's house, not even considering the very probable chance that he might not cooperate with them.

13

Friends Not-Ever

Bev washed down her cereal with a swig of milk right out of the jug, standing, as she did for most of her meals these days, next to the kitchen sink. Her mom came in, now dressed for the day.

"Oh, shoot, I was hoping to make you breakfast this morning," she said upon noticing Bev put her bowl in the dishwasher. "Too bad your dad has to work today; he can't see any of you kids play. And I'll have to go back and forth between your and Bob's games."

Bev didn't like the idea of Pops missing her games and her mom seeing only some of them. She wondered about Gary, assuming Jerry Jr. and Larry were working.

Gary glided in just then, chipper, whistling, and freshly showered. "I'm going to your games, Bev."

"You're in a fine mood," Bev noted. He grabbed the milk from her and chugged it.

"Gary!" their mom protested. "Use a glass, please."

"Mom, I have news for you. None of us kids have used a glass in years."

Bev smiled at him in appreciation for coming to her games. Even if it was in part to see Ann, which is what Bev suspected, it would be nice to have him there. She had quickly gotten used to playing on the same team with Bob, and having a brother around was cool. She didn't have to wonder if Bob was still mad at her for choosing the girls' team; she knew him well enough to expect he might be grumpy with her for days.

But a few minutes later, he came into the kitchen with a big smile on his face. "Well, good morning, fellow champions," he said charmingly.

Bev and Gary were wary. Bob took the milk carton from Gary and took a big swallow. "Mmm, tastes like backwash."

"Robert!" Mrs. Jenkins said, confiscating the milk, pulling a glass out of the cabinet, and pouring milk into it. She put the glass on the counter, where her children proceeded to ignore it.

Despite being suspicious of Bob's good mood, Bev soaked up this rare moment with half her family. On another Saturday in another era, they would all be eating her mother's pancakes while her pops sat at the head of the table, studying the paper. Sometimes he didn't work on Saturdays just so he could watch one of the boys' games or attend a Saturday afternoon theater or music program with his wife. Saturdays were always more laid-back, except, Bev suddenly realized, for her mother, who was always dressed and in full makeup preparing breakfast for everyone. Bev watched her mom now, while her brothers wrestled each other for the cereal box. Bev had always thought her mother was beautiful, even if it was just because she was her mom; but Bev noticed that recently, though her mother worked as hard outside the home, there was an ease about her. It con-firmed Bev's suspicions about the pressure of being a perfect housewife . . . and it confirmed Bev's desire to not be one.

Bob won the wrestling match and dumped some cereal into a bowl, then turned his attention to Bev. "Good luck today, Jen-kins." He smirked.

"Keep your luck, I don't need it. But thanks anyway, Jenkins," Bev retorted.

"Oh, and by the way, Diane Dunkelman is back on the team."

Ah, that's why Bob was acting so smug. "I heard something about that," Bev said.

"Seriously? After what she did?" Gary shook his head.

"You know, Jenkins, you would have made the same decision as I did. If you were honest, you'd admit that," Bev said to Bob.

"Hold up. You abandon your team for your own selfish gain and if I heard you right, you just accused *me* of being dishonest. Nice move." He slammed the cereal box on the counter, crum-pling the corner of the box. Gary snatched it before Bob tried to keep it away.

"You don't know what you're talking about," scoffed Bev, resisting playing the role she despised: picked-on little sister.

For all the good that was coming out of the future, Bev missed her family and missed being best friends with Bob. She wasn't too keen on the future-Bob. And she didn't like how future-Bob knew how to hit her right where it hurt: "Conrad Marshall's right about you. You're a user."

When Bev arrived at the softball field across town (driven by Gary, since, of course, Bob was headed elsewhere), she hadn't expected to be overcome by nerves. It wasn't her playing or the outcome of the games that she had misgivings about, but she was suddenly overcome with a queasy doubt that her old team might not welcome her back with open arms. Did they think that she had jumped ship for a chance to play baseball with the boys? Of course, no one knew that it had been her idea to get Diane back on the team. What had seemed like a splendid idea in the fervor of anger and zeal last night at midnight now seemed rash and nonsensical.

As she approached the field and dugout from the parking lot —an infinite distance to walk in front of all mankind—she wondered what had possessed her to convince Coach Rasmus to put Diane back on the team for the tournaments. Not only could she be perceived as thumbing her nose at Maxine, but Bev would have to contend with her rival in the close quarters of the same dugout again.

Diane hadn't always been as obnoxious as she was now. In junior high "last" year in 1953, when Bev and Diane had been on the same field hockey team, Diane had been a rival, but she hadn't been an enemy. The two had competed and pushed each other to do better and their team reaped the benefits. Partly in homage to another era, and partly to impel herself to outdo Diane, Bev had to have Diane play today. Instead of giving Diane the luxury of slinking off to lick her wounds in private while her actions were being investigated, Diane should be forced to contribute to a team, to perform under pressure and be seen, to answer to her peers.

Bev thought Diane's playing in the tournament was actually a tribute to Maxine, who was always looking to include and unify —and who, thanks to Diane, had herself been forced to own to her actions. Bev had learned more about teamwork from the Fifties Chix than she ever had from playing with her brothers or her field hockey team, softball team, or even the State-bound boys' baseball team. The Fifties Chix had lost everything familiar and stable, yet they had gained permanent friendships. She could probably even safely confide in them about her feelings for Conrad Marshall.

(What were her feelings for Conrad Marshall? She wished she could shut them off when he was acting like a spaz, but there they were, warm and sweet, tormenting and taunting her. She wondered where he was right at this moment. Was he fuming about her leaving the team? Or was it worse . . . was he not thinking of her at all?)

Bev had hoped to arrive before Diane to get her bearings with the team and settle in to what needed to be done. But halfway to the dugout, Bev realized she needn't have worried about everyone watching her return; all attention was on Diane, who had shown up early and was chatting nonstop while stretching. Even in the overcast, cloudy light, her hair sparkled. Her brief punishment had certainly done nothing to dampen her spirits . . . or her confidence. Bev shouldn't have been surprised that Diane presented herself with no contrition or shame, but she was disappointed anyway.

"Well, look who lowered herself to come back and play with the girls," Diane mocked upon spotting Bev.

Bev squinted and called back, "That's the difference between me and you, Dunkelman. I think I'm stepping it up to play with the girls."

Diane frowned, at a loss for a comeback. After a moment's hesitation, Diane quipped, "Bet you're surprised to see me back on the team."

The circle of softball players standing around Diane now looked to Bev for her retort. Their heads were on swivel, as if watching a charged tennis match. "I'll be *surprised* if you get chosen to play on the *national* team," Bev said as sweetly as possible. The other girls snickered, even Carla DiFrancisco, Diane's supposed best friend.

As she'd hoped, Diane's nostrils flared and her eyes narrowed with determination. Bev had Diane just where she wanted her: fired up and bent on bringing her best. Just like the pitcher Bev had hit her home run off of the night before.

14

Mission Impossible

Mary hadn't been comfortable on the walk to Twig's house. She wondered if James would think they were going behind his back; but, of course, she'd tried calling four times and had left messages. She also wondered how much luck they'd have with the cranky old custodian without James there to moderate. Once again, Judy had easily found the address and Mary reminded herself to get more familiar with the computer. It came in handy.

"James will understand," Ann soothed her nervous friend. "If we have less than a week for the *This is Your Life* assembly for Mrs. F, then we have to do this."

"It could be nothing. It could be a big bust, or it could answer our questions about Mrs. F, her friends, and the watch, and even give us more clues about time travel," Mary said, fanning herself in the morning heat. Her gloves and hat didn't help, but at least she only had to carry one of Mrs. F's old high school yearbooks, convincing the other girls to each take one. Still, she noted how quickly she had gotten accustomed to James driving her and her friends wherever they needed to go.

"I thought it was a great idea, but now that we're on our way, I'm not so sure. Can't we just ask Mrs. F about the watch? Or ask Aunt Row what she knows?" Maxine asked. She had lots of questions for Mrs. F. Like who was the girl Mrs. F had written about in *The Visible Truth*, the one who was a dancer and desperate to know the truth? Had Mrs. F been writing about herself poetically in the third person? As far as Maxine knew, even thinking back to 1955, then-Miss Boggs hadn't been a dancer.

"We can still talk to them, but maybe if we've done our homework ahead of time, we can ask the right questions and they won't be able to be so evasive," Mary insisted.

The girls giggled at Mary's incessant need to create "homework."

"It should be at the end of this street," Judy announced.

They stopped in front of the small, unremarkable gray ranch house with the tidy green lawn, perfectly trimmed hedges, and pruned trees. Except for the fact that it was three-dimensional, it could have been an architect's tidy, tightly-rendered sketch.

"This is it? I expected something more," Mary said, realizing she had built up this visit to epic proportions. As she did with a lot of things.

"Well, he is a school janitor," Judy said.

"According to James, he's been a lot of other things, too," Maxine reminded them.

"Now or never," sighed Ann, urging them to the door. "We've got a game we don't want to be late to."

Mary led the charge to the front door, remembering the last time they'd done something like this; it had been to Aunt Row's, and James had unexpectedly answered the door. She had a brief crazy fancy that James would open the door here, too. After several minutes, it was clear James wouldn't be answering their knocking and Mary was doubting Twigler would either.

Just when they started to pass the questioning *Should we give up?* looks to each other, the door swung open.

Twigler looked different in his everyday clothes—handsome, almost, Mary thought. His hooded eyes were dark gray but alert, and small tufts of hair circled the bottom half of his head like smoke rings. He was trim and barely taller than Ann, wearing a plaid shirt and a coordinating cardigan, despite the heat. He had the nicely manicured hands of someone who did not clean up the mess of teenagers day in and day out.

"Hi, Mr. Twigler, we're—"

"I know who you are. Let me guess, you're not selling cookies."

The girls laughed politely. Mary said, "We're doing a project for school—a tribute to Mrs. Fairview and we understand you went to school with her. If you don't mind, we'd like to—"

"Nosy little generation, aren't you?" Twig muttered.

"I beg your pardon?" Ann said as sweetly as possible.

"Never mind. Come on in. But I don't have all day."

Mary had second thoughts about going into a strange (in more ways than one) old man's house and wouldn't have considered it without her friends with her. She grasped Maxine's and Judy's hands, Ann grabbed Judy's, and the four of them ventured into Twig's living room.

Just as tidy as the yard outside, the room was reminiscent of Mrs. F's apartment above Row's garage: no personal effects and a drab color palette. Mary shifted into sleuth mode, noting the lack of ornamentation as a clue. Maybe Twig had a big mansion hidden away somewhere else?

Twig gestured at the furniture for the girls to sit, then, forgoing any niceties, said, "Well? What?"

Mary stayed calm, cool, and unhurried and the others followed her lead. They crowded onto his light brown sofa.

"Do you live here alone? I mean, do you have a family or children?" Judy asked.

"Yes, I live alone. No family," Twig said.

"Do you have any pets?"

"Look, I've got a lot to do today. Why don't we get right to it?"

The girls seriously doubted Twig had "a lot to do," but they didn't want to blow their chances. He seemed irritable enough to start with without their further irking him by asking unnecessary personal questions.

"We brought these yearbooks," Mary said and they each held out a book. "Maybe they would be a great place to start."

He didn't make a move to take the books. Instead he rubbed his face with both hands as if his head hurt. "You have any specific questions you'd like to ask?"

"Yes," Maxine spoke up. "Who's this girl?" She crossed to where he stood near the doorway to the kitchen and opened her yearbook.

"Says right here: Emily Jackson," Twig said after a noticeable pause.

"Oh, right," Maxine said smoothly as if she hadn't noticed. "Did you know her?"

Mary wished Maxine would ask open-ended questions, feeling she should have better prepped the girls for this meeting, but she kept her mouth shut.

"Obviously, I went to school with her. Yes, I knew her. Nice girl. Everyone liked her. Your friend Beverly Jenkins's uncle was quite keen on her."

As Mary digested this interesting tidbit, she was disconcerted by the fact that Twig knew that the five of them were friends. Granted, he was at school every day, but there was no reason they should have stood out in a school as overly populated as theirs. She thought better of following up with that line of reasoning since he was starting to talk about Emily Jackson.

"Wow, what a small world!" Maxine said brightly, attempting to use sheer, cheerful will to prompt Twig to continue. "And she was friends with Miss Boggs?"

"You mean Mrs. Fairview?" Twig said pointedly.

Maxine's face warmed but she tried not to falter. "Back then, I suppose she was Miss Boggs, wasn't she?"

Twig's doubtful glare lingered. "I suppose. No one called her that, I imagine, until she started teaching. Anyway, Emily was friends with Marion."

"Whatever happened to her?" Judy piped up.

"She left in the middle of the school year; just up and disappeared."

Now the girls grew restless; this was not a piece of information they had heard about. "Was she a dancer?" Maxine asked suddenly.

He nodded.

"And she and Miss Boggs were friends with Rowena Nolan?" Maxine pressed.

Twig took a small step back, so subtle a movement it might have gone unnoticed, but not to Mary. He was getting spooked. They needed to tread lightly. They were finally getting a new round of answers . . . or about to. Just then Mary heard a familiar voice from the other room.

"Reggie. Watch!"

Mary jumped up impulsively, forgetting her strategy to be delicate. "That's Ike! Mrs. F's bird!"

Now Twigler was uncomfortable. "Oh, is it? I'll have to tell her. The bird flew into my yard last week and he wouldn't leave me alone, so I let him in and fed him."

Mary was emboldened. She stepped forward until she was standing next to Maxine and facing the old man directly. "Is there something you can tell us, you know, for Mrs. F's celebration? Or anything else we should know?"

Twigler's hard expression and mannerisms melted and he made his way to a nearby chair. He looked old all of a sudden. "I don't know. There was a time when I could have known, but not now. I'm just biding my time."

"Until what?" Ann asked.

He jerked his head up and glared at her, his hardened appearance back in full force. "Until I find out what this has all been for."

"Reggie watch!" Ike screeched.

Twig hadn't expected to feel empathy for the girls, but he had. They'd looked so eager, nervous . . . and *young* out there on his door step. He had stood leaning against the door for a long time listening to the rap-tap-tap of their knuckles until his curiosity had gotten the best of him. *Curiosity killed the cat,* his foster mom had liked to say. He wished it would kill that dang bird in the other room. He had taken a deep breath and opened the door.

The girls had collectively gasped, eyes widened in surprise, when he'd actually answered their incessant knocking. He had found himself irritated by their naiveté and hopefulness. Just what did they think he could do for them that their faces were saturated in such dewy expectation? He'd thought of the last time he must have looked like that and knew without having to search his memories that it was when Rowena Nolan had come into the shop with that "broken" watch.

In one moment, everything had come together, all points of light like a laser beam singularly focused. But instead of melding all the jagged pieces of his life into one smooth whole, it had further splintered it, permanently severing his destiny from his desire.

15

Accidental Matchmaker

Gary parked the car and brought his laptop with him to the stands. He'd probably get mocked for bringing homework to Bev's tournaments, but he had limited time to complete his AP History paper and he wouldn't have been able to concentrate at home anyway, knowing Bev was playing and Ann was watching. So he figured he might as well get some work done before the crowds (i.e., Ann) showed up. He wondered what kind of support the girls' games would get with the boys' team playing simultaneously.

The school where the tournament was being held was a new, featureless, cement eyesore that reminded him of the home improvement chain where his dad worked. There were no mature trees to be seen, almost like they had dropped the school and athletic fields onto a flat, boring patch of desert. The few saplings that dotted the perimeter were a sorry excuse for landscaping, each sporting a dozen leaves at the most. Gary wondered how one could be inspired by a place like this and thought of all that Irina had told him about the rich, varied history of beautiful Belgrade. He decided he'd visit the city as soon as possible, maybe even find a way to study there during college.

And of course take Ann with him.

He rolled his eyes at himself and opened his laptop, setting a goal of writing 700 words of his paper before Ann arrived.

He put on his sunglasses to better see the computer screen. *Dear Irina*, he wrote instead.

Ann and her friends thanked Bitsy for the ride and hurried around the school to the fields in back.

"I hope we're not too late to get good seats," Maxine said.

Judy managed a "Me, too." They all knew Judy was restraining herself from complaining that she was missing Bob's games, and at the ideal time when she wouldn't have to compete with Diane Dunkelman for Bob's attention, too. Though she still sounded strained, she had put on her best cheerful attitude and had asked her mom to drive them to Bev's tournament after they had gone to Twig's house.

Mary was distracted also, not just from the meeting with Twig, but because she'd been unable to reach James to ask him to accompany them to the custodian's house.

Ann surmised that Mary was more anxious about James's whereabouts than insecure about their relationship. James would have been the first person to want to confront Twig about his knowledge of time travel, but he hadn't answered his phone or responded to the message Mary left. Ann thought of

Gary Jenkins then and an unexpected bounce came into her step as she wondered if he'd be at Bev's tournament.

"Oh," Maxine said as they all stopped in their tracks.

"I thought we were late. Where is everyone?" Mary said.

The stands were sparsely populated and the energy that had been so prolific at the boys' game last night was decidedly absent here.

Ann couldn't stop her eyes from roving the bleachers; she spotted Gary and felt some relief.

"Isn't this the future? I mean, I thought more people would be interested in girls' games," Judy said with an edge of pout in her voice that hinted at, *After all, I came when I could have been watching the boys.*

"And James isn't here, either," murmured Mary.

"There's Bev pitching." Judy pointed and the girls made their way to join the few spectators.

Gary sat up straighter and tossed an eager look Ann's way.

"Wanna sit with him?" Maxine said. Ann was grateful to be asked this time instead of compelled by everyone else. She nodded.

She slid in next to Gary, who looked rather appealing in his sunglasses and a green shirt. She tried to ignore the fact that Judy, Mary, and Maxine all proceeded to start a quiet conversation while intentionally excluding her so she could focus on Gary. She found it at once irritating and sweet.

"What did we miss?" Ann asked Gary.

"Second inning; no score, Bev's been pitching, left two runners stranded."

"How's her arm after pitching last night?"

"Oh, she's pitching underhand today, so there's not as much strain as pitching baseball. Either way, she's pretty powerful. There are the scouts." Gary pointed at two women and a man sitting near each other several rows down.

"You think she'll get chosen?" Ann said.

"Unless they're blind and ignorant," declared Gary. Then he quickly changed the subject, as if the game were a mere formality. "So, I'm glad to see you. I emailed Irina last night. Thanks again for her contact info."

Ann swallowed. Her throat felt constricted for some reason. "Don't worry if she doesn't write back right away; she's several hours—"

"—seven hours ahead, I know. We emailed each other all night until she had to go to work. We would have IMed but she was having trouble with her connection. Well, you know how it is."

"Sure," Ann said. But she wasn't sure.

"Anyway, she was so helpful! And really fun to write with; now I know why you guys are so close even though you've never met in person."

Ann didn't know if she should be jealous of or happy for Gary or Irina, but she didn't like the chill that came over her, even as the temperature rose outside. She hastily reviewed all that she'd ever written Irina, trying to recall if she'd ever mentioned Gary by name. When she didn't respond because she couldn't find something positive or encouraging to gush, Gary kept talking. "I learned all about the wars from a firsthand observer, you know, someone really affected by it all. And when she was a child no less. She even told me about how her mom—your Aunt Zaria—

was killed by the NATO bombings. That must have been hard on the whole family."

It had been. In World War II. Ann didn't know how Aunt Zaria had been killed this time around, but in 1941, Yugoslavia had fought to resist the invasion of Hitler's Third Reich. Ann's Uncle David (on her mom's side), Irina's father, had been a soldier who survived the "Short War" which had unfortunately claimed Aunt Zaria and Ann's other uncles on her dad's side, Akim and Alexei. Ann's family had been decimated along with the Jewish population of then-Yugloslavia. As Gary continued his excited rant, the injustice of it all, which so often lay dormant in her, began to bubble up in Ann.

"It's not fair!" Ann interrupted Gary's mini-lecture on the inevitability of the Yugoslav Wars in the 1990s. "NATO was formed to stem communism, but communism only grew to stem Hitler's fascism. And NATO bombings killed my aunt? It's not fair!"

Gary grew silent and the few people in the stands, including Maxine, Judy and Mary looked startled at Ann's rising voice.

"I know. That's kind of the thesis of my paper," Gary said quietly. "If you're interested in reading it . . . . I'm not done yet, but—"

"Of course I'd like to see it," Ann said, calming herself. Maybe Gary's paper would help her understand what had happened to Yugoslavia-now-Serbia from 1955 to present day.

Gary reached down to his messenger bag leaning against his leg and pulled out his laptop. "You can take a look at it now, if you want." He put the computer in her lap and opened it.

Ann scanned the screen and realized she was looking at a long letter. "Dear Irina?" she said.

Gary turned a deep shade of red and fumbled for the computer. "Oh, sorry. I didn't realize that—well, anyway, I can let you read my paper when it's done. I'll email it—oh, Irina says you don't prefer email. I can print it off for you."

"That's fine," Ann said. With great effort, she turned her attention to the game. She was here to see Bev, not be a matchmaker for her cousin and Bev's geeky older brother Gary. Gary put the computer away and they fell into another uneasy silence.

Maybe, Ann told herself, she wouldn't be as frazzled if she hadn't just come from that exasperating meeting with Mr. Twigler.

16

The Gift

"Tommy, I was hoping I'd find you here," Row said. She'd gussied herself up, lipstick and all. Twig wished she'd come in her overalls.

He hid the book he had been sent, shoving it carelessly and hurriedly under the cash register. He asked after her with a reserved politeness—reserved because he wanted to ask why she hadn't returned his calls.

"I heard Marion Boggs is engaged to be married," Twig said in as conversational a tone as he could muster.

"News travels fast." Row nodded.

"Good news, I hope."

"Of course." Row smiled and feigned interest in the dusty items in the shop.

"What brings you in today?" Twig asked after a beat.

"It's awkward," Row told him, asking if they might be able to speak somewhere more private. Ignoring the fact that they were utterly alone in the shop and most likely would be until closing, Twig courageously asked if they should meet after for dinner. He knew his cheeks flushed when she agreed, but he otherwise maintained his composure. He knew he was pushing his luck when he asked if he should pick her up.

"Oh, no, we can meet there," Row said casually. His heart seized. Her carefree disposition reminded him of the lighthearted teenaged girl he used to tease on her front porch; but her informality insisted that their dinner date was nothing more than a meeting.

After she left, he had two hours until meeting Row for dinner, but after twenty minutes of reading the same sentence in his book and not being able to focus on the proposal that had been sent along with it, he decided to find a hands-on activity that would require his full attention. He was grateful for the rusted-out motor of the antique grandfather clock that had recently been brought in. He savored the irony of trying to get time back up and running and how quickly the time passed while he did it. He found himself wondering in those circumstances who the master was: man or time. He would find out soon enough.

At last, the functioning clocks told him it was time for dinner and he tucked his reading material—a top-secret proposal and part of his future—into the safe, spinning the lock two extra times. He flipped the shop's sign to "closed," locked the door, and walked to the restaurant whistling. The early summer air had not yet lost its charm to the dreaded humidity of July and Twig waved a hearty hello to passersby.

Row was waiting for him even though he was early. He found her eagerness encouraging. When the host offered to seat them near the front window (which was fine with Twig if friends and neighbors spotted him having supper with a beauty), Row asked for a more private table. Twig bit his tongue when he was tempted to make a remark about it, remembering that of late, she had not been responsive to his sarcasm.

After ordering, Row retrieved her pocketbook. As she clutched it, she leaned across the table toward Twig and spoke in quiet tones. "I need a favor, Tommy, but I need to know if I can trust you first."

"Of course you can," he said, happy to be needed and eager to be trusted. Her eyes sparkled along with the gold heart locket she always wore around her neck like a landmark, reminding him that this was the girl he'd known for years and that though she'd grown into a woman, her Row-ness remained undiluted.

"I know I can trust you, but . . . I mean really trust you."

"Oh, really trust—"

"I'm serious, Tommy."

When it came to Row, he liked being called Tommy instead of "Twig," and it helped him focus. "You really can, I promise," he said sincerely, unaware at the time of what a lie it was.

Row looked him in the eye for what seemed a day but was probably only ten seconds and then opened her clutch, pulling out a velvet pouch. "This is a very special piece that needs fixing." She glanced around the restaurant before sliding out a beautiful antique gold watch.

In all his years working at the shop and going to conventions with his pop, Twig had never seen a watch like it. He knew at a glance that the face was crystal and immediately noticed an oddity: there were two second hands and one was nearly invisible, it was turning so swiftly. He blinked in case he was seeing it wrong.

"Where did you—"

"Now Twig, listen," she insisted, as his spirits plummeted at being called Twig again. "This watch is probably unlike any you've ever seen. And it needs, uh, fixing, but not to tell time, per se . . . ." Her voice drifted off as Twig's heart picked up speed.

"Whose watch is this, Row? I can't be working on something that you—you don't have authority to—"

"Oh for Pete's sake, I didn't steal it, if that's what you're asking. Well, I didn't exactly steal it. It's Marion's. I'm borrowing it to get it fixed. As a wedding present for her. She used to wear it all the time, wouldn't go without it, and lately she hasn't been using it—I mean, wearing it—so I think it may be broken."

Twig tried to respond, but no words came out. He took a sip of water, spilling some down the side of his glass. He tugged at the knot in his tie to give himself more room to breathe.

This had to be a test. He knew that upon completing his application, there would be a thorough background check by the FBI and plenty of questioning. He'd heard horror stories about just how extensive it would be. Could this be part of their procedure, calling in someone from his past like Row, to see how he would handle it? He would make calls tomorrow to find out. For now, he would play it cool and relish a dinner date—meeting—with Rowena Nolan.

The waiter came by with a lit candle, placing it between them and giving them a knowing look. The way Row swiftly and nervously covered the watch with her napkin told Twig that she wasn't being put up to this. He couldn't believe his dumb luck. That meant the very watch that Reginald Fairview had based his theories on was falling right into Twig's lap; and by Row of all people.

It was the start of the rest of his life.

17

Drama Queens

Conrad had avoided his mother long enough and knew she could not be put off any longer.

When she offered to pick him up for breakfast and then take him to his game that morning, he said yes. It was his own stupid fault, he reminded himself. If he hadn't been out with Bev last night after the game, he could have given his mother a hug then and been off the hook this morning. He dutifully said a prayer for his team to play their best, thinking briefly of including his mom and sibs, but put it off for tomorrow in church. He intentionally did not think of Beverly Jenkins. At all. Except to remind himself to not think of her.

"I'm working the swing shift, but I'll be at your morning game!" his dad, TJ, called as Conrad headed out to meet his mom in the parking lot. He hoped she wouldn't honk. It was an apartment complex and people were probably still sleeping. It would be just like her to honk, and everyone and their dog would look out the window and see Conrad and blame him.

"How's your dad?" she said when he climbed in the front seat. No "Good morning" or "How are you?".

"Fine." Conrad gave his standard answer.

"And how's my boy?" Conrad hated when she referred to him like that; it reminded him of a mom's normal affection for her son.

"Fine," he replied. His mom ignored his stoniness.

They went to a chain restaurant with terrible food; not that Conrad cared. He wasn't picky about what he ate as long as it was edible and there was a lot of it. As he shoveled mouthfuls of syrup-soaked pancakes, eggs, and sausage in swift movements from his plate to his face, his mom sipped coffee and chatted about his siblings.

In between bites, he asked about them. He missed them, no matter how unruly and wild things got when they were all together.

"Ginny's taking ballet and she's really quite talented," Conrad's mom said.

Conrad gulped a half a glass of orange juice at once. "That must make Auntie happy."

"You know it!"

"How is she?"

"She's thinking of retiring, selling the studio."

"Auntie Em? Are you serious?" Conrad paused to wipe his mouth with his napkin and take a breath. "What would she do instead?"

"I'm trying to convince her to move back here. With me. But you know how—"

Conrad dropped his napkin and slumped into his side of the booth. He hadn't meant for it to be his reaction, but he couldn't hide it in time. His mom's face fell.

"Would it be that awful, baby? To have your mama and your family here with you?"

"I have family here."

"You know what I mean." Her brown eyes—the same color and depth that Conrad had inherited—shimmered with tears and she looked away.

Suddenly, Conrad felt like he'd eaten too much and his belly felt cramped. "I know what you meant, Ma. It's just that I'm so busy and I don't know how much I'd even get to see y'all. I'm getting a job this summer and I'm working on getting scholarships—"

She nodded, but didn't look his way. That stiff upper lip act that she had going really got to him. There was only one other person who could make him feel this bad.

And she was taking the field right about now.

Bev wished for the energy she'd had last night, but everything felt like a real drag instead of an inspiration. Her friends were absent from the stands—she knew they must still be meeting with Mr. Twigler, but that didn't make her feel any better; Diane Dunkelman was being more petty than Bev had ever imagined and was focused entirely on herself instead of the team; and Conrad was mad at her. She blocked with all her might the thought that she had made the wrong decision.

She had to admit that winning last night hadn't ridden solely on her talent. She had her dad and brothers to thank for pushing her to improve, and she had the teammates who had believed in her and played well in their own right. Even the Vikings got some credit for riling her up with their stupid lipstick stunt. She didn't know what it would be, but she needed something today. Otherwise, the scouts would dismiss her, the team could lose the tournament, and worst of all, she would have missed going to State with the baseball team. It was her own darned fault; she had convinced Coach Rasmus to let Diane back on the team— and it had taken a lot of convincing.

"Jenkins, you know we can't do that," Coach had said on the phone last night.

"What she is accused of is wrong . . . and it was to one of my best friends, so believe me, I'm not Dunkelman's biggest fan."

Coach had been confused and there had been a long pause on the phone as she had tried to work out why Bev—a favorite target of Diane's—would be requesting that Diane rejoin the team.

"Coach, Diane is good—one of the best players we have. Why should the team get punished while she gets to sit it out and act like the victim?"

"I'll consider what you're saying, but it's not my decision alone to make. I'll have to get Principal Jones on the phone, and who knows if that will happen at this late hour."

Bev had thanked Coach for considering it, marveling at herself. She had just blown her own chances of having a blissful, Diane Dunkelman-free softball tournament.

"Thank you, Beverly, for being a team player. No matter what happens tomorrow, you're a winner for looking out for the team."

Now, as Bev stretched her pitching arm by slinging some balls to Carla DiFrancisco, Dunkelman strutted around, flinging her glossy blond ponytail like she was on the catwalk and laughing secretly with Lacy Garritson. Lacy, who, last night, had been all too ready to be done with Diane. Focusing her attention back on DiFrancisco, Bev found herself missing Marsalis and his smirk.

"Rethinking defending Dunkelman, are ya?" Carla called.

Bev wanted to pitch a fastball that would erase DiFrancisco's smug little smile, but instead, she said, "Hold up," and jogged over to Diane. "Can I talk to you a minute?"

The team focused all their attention on the two of them—or refocused from just Diane to include Beverly, as the case was.

"I'm the captain, Jenkins," Diane said nonsensically.

"Fine . . . can I talk to the captain in private?"

"OooOOOOooo," Diane jeered as her friends snickered. But fortunately Diane stepped away with Bev before she could yank Diane's pony tail as Bob and her other brothers had done to her on so many occasions.

"Look, I know you like to be in the spotlight. We have that in common, at least when it comes to the field." Bev remembered what she'd said to Conrad last night before the game about drama. "And you and I have a history of competition, but I'm asking you for a favor. You don't owe me one, I just want us both to get what we want. We need to create some drama."

"What are you even talking about?" Diane chomped her gum in concentration, her eyebrows furrowed in disdain. But at least she was listening and not posing and performing for her flunkies.

"Can we take our need to be the best on the field and create some drama for the other team? Let's give the scouts something to see. The team needs you; let's use our edge to make the whole team be better. Maybe we'll all get on the national team."

"Dream on, Jenkins!" Diane snorted. "Whatever, can we get back to warming up?"

"Fine." Bev walked away, shaking her head.

"Jenkins?"

"What?" Bev didn't look back.

"When you're all washed up as a player, which will probably be, like, tomorrow, you'd make a pretty good coach."

Bev averted her grin. "Well, you'll be a great water girl. Why don't you practice now and go get me some?"

"Whatever," Dunkelman said. But Bev could hear the smile in her voice, too.

When, in the second inning, Bev noticed the arrival of her friends, she was already feeling more like herself: determined, energized, and certain. She only wished she could feel like that off the field. But one thing at a time; first, she had a softball team and some scouts to inspire.

"Let's go, Bev!" hollered Diane Dunkelman from the outfield.

Bev didn't even pretend it was Conrad's voice.

18

Third Time, No Charm

Twig had, of course, lied. He'd told the four girls who'd come calling that he had a full day planned. His life was as empty as ever. The yard and house were as clean as they were going to get for the moment and he had finished reading the latest science fiction novel he'd checked out from the library.

He fed Ike. It wasn't the first time Ike had come around. The bird had escaped before and come and found him. Strange. If he believed in that kind of thing, he might think the bird was a messenger, especially since the bird's favorite phrase to squawk was "Reggie watch!"—the two things Twig wished he could blame for his downfall.

Ridiculous. The bird no more had a message for him than the watch was responsible for time travel. He'd managed to prove that over and over again during more than thirty years' research at Montauk Air Force base in New York, to the chagrin of the US military.

After Row gave him the watch at dinner that fateful June evening in 1955, he raced back to the shop and let himself back in, keeping the sign on "closed." First, he studied the outside of the watch detail by detail, and made notes as he always did for when he needed to take a piece apart and put it back together. He even photographed it from every angle and considered not taking it apart until he could have the film developed to make sure he'd gotten good enough photographs. But, though he'd been patient a good part of his life, this part was not to be included. He couldn't wait.

With the doors locked tight, the blinds drawn, and nothing but a bright single spotlight shining over the gleaming gold timepiece on his work table, he set to work to open it up. The back popped off and he held his breath, waiting for an implosion or explosion or some version of a wormhole to suck him into it. But nothing happened.

In fact, nothing happened the rest of the night as he took the watch apart piece by piece. By dawn, he had put it back together twice and dismantled it a third time to discover that, other than the 18-karat gold the watch consisted of (which was something in and of itself; he'd never seen a watch run on parts all made of gold), there was nothing remarkable about the mechanics inside the piece. No secret time machine hidden inside, no genie that popped out to grant time travel wishes. He had noticed that there was only one second hand, no matter where he looked, but as soon as the watch was closed up again, the other one appeared. He speculated that it was traveling the speed of light and made plans to find a way to measure the speed.

He also wrote down—and planned to ask his foster brother, who spoke a little German, to translate—the inscription on the back of the watch: Liebe kann nicht nach der Zeit enthalten sein. Die Liebe ist ewig.

Over the next month, Twig disassembled and reassembled the watch several times a day. Never could he find a motor for the mysterious second hand—or find the other second hand itself if the watch wasn't fully assembled. It only appeared when the back was attached and all pieces were in place.

So when Row came back to the shop, he'd almost entirely forgotten where he'd obtained the watch in the first place. He'd been in the back room, simply staring at that whirring second hand after rebuilding the watch for what felt like the millionth time. He had wanted his answers before accepting his new job, but it was looking like there would be no new job. Bells on the door clanged against each other and the glass pane of the door and he heard a lady's voice call out, "Hello?"

He didn't even recognized her voice, he'd been so distracted.

"Tommy." She addressed him the way he preferred when he appeared from out of the back room.

"Row?" he said in surprise. He'd guiltily grabbed a silver watch on his way to the front of the store, wanting to appear productive, paranoid about his obsession over one singular timepiece when others needed his attention. He had called Row a week after having the watch, wrestling with his conscience. His conscience once again reared its head upon seeing her in person. "I tried to call—"

"I know." Row straightened her hat. There was a formality about her that was unnatural, a distance that made Twig's heart ache. She said curtly, "I want the watch back."

Twig felt panic expanding in his chest. He cleared his throat. "It's busted, you said so yourself."

"You and I both know it's not broken, Twig. What did you do with it? I want it back. I brought something in trade."

"What is it?" It didn't matter what it was unless it was another watch, but Twig had to see what Row was willing to give up to get the watch back.

She presented a gold necklace and glittering heart-shaped pendant in her gloved palm. Twig recognized it right away. Row had always worn it. Now, her neck looked empty. Maybe that's why she looked so different to him.

"It's beautiful, to be sure, but—" Twig held the locket up to inspect it, a cursory glance. He would never take something like that from her, even if it was in trade.

Row explained how valuable the locket was, telling Twig with a catch in her voice that she couldn't afford to pay for the repair— what she probably meant was she couldn't afford to pay enough to convince him to give it back if he'd figured out what it could do. In exchange, she said, she could offer her most precious possession in the whole world.

"It really is broken," Twig said, unable to look her in the eye. "I took it apart and have tried to fix it. Twice," he lied.

"You know what they say," Row said in a forced cheerful tone.

"What's that?"

"Third time's a charm."

"Is that what you'd say if I asked you on another date, Rowena?" Twig hadn't meant to be so direct. But he was suddenly aware of what their relationship had become—or maybe what it had always been. One-sided and doomed.

"Can you please just get the watch back to me in one piece?"

The door rattled and Rowena jumped.

Reggie Fairview strutted in and Twig panicked.

"Well, hello there, Row," Reggie said in that charming, confident rich-boy manner that was second nature to him.

"Reggie. What brings you in here?"

"Looking for a gift for Marion, of course. Twig, good to see you, friend."

"You, too, Mr. Fairview," Twig knew he sounded stilted, especially compared to Reggie. He turned to Row. "Maybe we can talk about this over dinner, Row?"

"I'm not going out with you, Tommy. I just want my—the—watch back."

Twig's ego took a hit in front of unruffled, debonair Reggie, who ignored the slight and said smoothly, "What watch is that? Let's see it, Twig."

Twig excused himself to the back room and picked up the watch, deciding what he should do. If Row saw that he brought out another watch, she would say so and Twig would look like he was hiding something from both of them. He assured himself he didn't need to keep the watch from Reggie anyway; it was, after all, ultimately his bride's watch and Reggie would be the last person to announce his intentions with the watch.

But besides all that, returning the watch would be severing the only connection he had with Row. In that instant, he was making a major life decision. Only weeks ago, he thought he could have it all, now he was choosing which broken half of him to discard. With a trembling hand, he reached for the burgundy felt and gingerly laid the watch on it. He said a silent good-bye to Row and to the life he'd hoped they could have together and walked slowly back to the sales area.

"It doesn't look broken," she challenged when he reappeared. But had she been paying attention, she would have known what it was that was broken: his heart.

"Why, that's Marion's watch," Reggie said, his voice as honeyed as ever.

"I brought it in to get it fixed," Row rushed to say.

"It looks good as new. Why can't she have it, Twig?"

Twig didn't appreciate being put on the spot. Reggie knew exactly why Twig was reluctant to give it up. "She—she said she couldn't pay for it." Twig felt foolish and ungentlemanlike. How quickly he had thrown Row under the bus after giving up on a life with her.

"I'm happy to pay for it. You're giving it back to May, right, Rowena? How much, Twig?"

Twig wanted to laugh. How much for giving up Row and the watch? There was no number big enough.

Reggie said, "Twig is starting a new business and I'm going to be an investor. That's why I came in, Tommy; to tell you the good news. And now Marion's getting her watch back, too. What a grand day."

"It is, Mr. Fairview. Thank you," Twig pulled out Row's hand. He smiled so that he wouldn't cry, knowing he was touching her hand for the last time. In it, he put her locket and the gold watch. "No charge."

The memory still pained Twig after all this time. Now, fifty-five years later, standing alone with a chatty bird, it dawned on him why all his research and development had failed and why his life had come up empty. He realized in less time than it takes to draw in a breath what the motor was that kept that mysterious hand running, what had kept Row and Marion friends all these years, what had brought the girls to his door that morning. No complex mathematical equation, scientific research, or exposition of physical law could possibly come close to explaining the component that made that watch tick and that had eluded him his whole life.

It was love.

As his foster brother had translated, the inscription of the watch was all Twig had ever needed to know all along: *Love cannot be contained by time. Love is forever.*

19

Boys to Men

YOU KNOW HOW YOU KNOW SOMETHING—SUPER-FICIALLY—AND THEN SOMETHING HAPPENS AND THEN YOU KNOW IT KNOW IT?

I ALWAYS KNEW THAT A TEAM WAS ONLY AS GOOD AS ITS MEMBERS. BLAH BLAH BLAH. NOW I KNOW WHAT THAT MEANS. I'M WRITING YOU AS STATE CHAMP!!!! WE DID IT!!!

DISTRICT CHAMPIONSHIP WAS CAKE—WE POUNDED THEM HANDILY 6-1. ALMOST FELT BAD FOR THEM. ALMOST. I GOT 3 RBIS AND A HOMER, AND CAUGHT A LINE DRIVE THAT WAS COMING TO TAKE MY HEAD CLEAN OFF. EXCEPT FOR JENKINS ACTING LIKE A BABY—

AND I MEAN BOB JENKINS—IT WAS A SWEET
GAME. (THAT BOY WAS MADE FOR DUNKELMAN.
TOGETHER THEY CAN THROW A HISSY FIT AND
RAISE IT AND SEND IT TO COLLEGE ON
SCHOLARSHIP.)

OTHER THAN JENKINS, IT WAS BEAUTIFUL, LIKE
I SAID. EXCEPT FOR ONE OTHER THING.

THAT ONE OTHER THING MISSING REALLY
STOOD OUT IN THE STATE GAME, BUT I FELT IT IN
THE SEMIS TOO. MAYBE IT WAS BECAUSE WE
ONLY HAD AN HOUR IN BETWEEN GAMES OR
MAYBE IT WAS BECAUSE WE WERE SWEATING
LIKE A BEAST, BUT THE ENERGY WAS GONE IN
THAT SECOND GAME. AND THERE WAS NOBODY
TO GET US PUMPED UP. THERE WAS TOO MUCH
TIME BETWEEN THE ACTION—WHICH MEANT TOO
MUCH TIME TO THINK. YEAH, WE WON. BUT IT
WAS UGLY.

IF BEVERLY JENKINS HAD BEEN THERE, IT
WOULD HAVE BEEN PERFECT. WHICH IS WHY
AFTER WE WON, I CONVINCED A BUNCH OF THE
GUYS TO GO WITH ME TO CHECK OUT THE GIRLS'
GAMES.

PEACE OUT - STATE CHAMP!!! C.M.

Conrad decided to write more tomorrow. Or not. Sometimes he just wanted to soak up the moment and not write about it. He didn't shove the journal under his mattress this time; he just tossed it on his desk, leaned back in his chair, and smiled.

To: <Irina Brajer>
From: <Gary Jenkins>
Date: May 29, 6:20 pm
Subject: RE: re: Favor for Ann's friend?

Hi Irina,

It's me again. I just wanted to thank you for your help with my paper . . . and for talking to me about Ann. I wish you could meet her in person (I'm sure you will soon). She's talented, kind, smart, funny (but the best kind of funny because she doesn't know that she is). If you haven't seen her paintings, I'm attaching one for you. It's a painting she did for a friend

Delete. Delete. Delete. Delete. Gary sighed. What was he doing? He was procrastinating writing his paper, but he was procrastinating something else, too. Instead of telling Ann how he felt, he was telling her cousin, a girl halfway around the world whom he'd never met. It was cowardice. He was taking an elementary school strategy of telling Ann's friend so that Irina would tell Ann. He might as well get out a blank sheet of paper and write, "Do you like me? Yes / No," and provide check boxes.

He considered this a moment, then gave himself his own mental check box and said "No!" out loud. He had dropped Bev off after the tournament at that fifties diner and was going to pick her up later. Maybe he could just show up a few minutes—or an hour—earlier to see Ann in person?

He grabbed his keys and shut the laptop. His AP World History paper could wait.

Bob knew he needed to get a hold of himself. He was blowing this game. The harder he tried to hang on, the more quickly it slipped through his fingers like dry, fine, slippery sand. He called on all the years of coaching by his dad and Larry and Jerry, Jr. But it was his little sister's image that came to mind.

He pitched. Ball three. That was his best stuff! He shook his head and Marsalis stared him down. *I know, I know*, he said to his catcher without speaking.

He stepped back in place on the mound, took a deep short breath, and threw. Ball four. The bases were loaded now. He slapped his glove on his thigh in frustration and instantly Marsalis was there.

"Don't do it, dude. Stay with us. This is State." Marsalis looked him in the eye trying to calm him, but Bob looked away.

He wanted to screech and whine, throw a tantrum as if he were a two-year-old. But he knew that wouldn't get them out of this inning unscathed—it would certainly get him thrown out of the game. He just wasn't feeling it, and there was nothing worse in the world than standing on that mound and having nothing left. He was tapped. But it was too soon for relief; he didn't want that either.

"How do you think the girls' team is doing?" Bob mumbled.

"Is that what this is about? Man, you wanna find out about the girls' games? Then strike out the next six batters so we can go see for ourselves."

Coach eyeballed them; did Bob need to come out?

"Girl up, man. Pitch like your sister." Marsalis hit Bob on the shoulder, flashed him a wicked smile, and ran back to his warn little spot behind home plate.

Bob didn't feel any less peeved, but now his negative energy was focused. He struck out the next three batters, leaving the runners stranded and miraculously getting his team out of the inning without further damage.

Mopping his face with an already dirty towel in the dugout, he heard his phone vibrate in his gym bag. No phones allowed in the dugout, but Coach was preoccupied, so Bob left the phone in his bag, but switched it on where he could still see it. Maybe it was an update on the girls' game from Diane. He didn't want to cave in, but his curiosity got the best of him.

Bob, I am so sorry to be missing your games. And I know everyone else is, too, your brother and Diane. She is doing a swell job and so is your sister. Just wanted you to know we are all thinking of you. From Judy.

PS. Sorry, it's Judy again. I got your text numbers from Gary. - Judy

He laughed out loud. Marsalis looked over at him and he tucked the phone back. How about that? He was getting a little support. He was being thought of. It felt nice to get a message from someone who wasn't texting just to remind him of how great she was.

Bob stood up and went to the railing as Bev had done the previous night. "Let's go, Marshall!" he called to Conrad, who was at bat.

James forgot to turn off his phone and fumbled with it to silence it, noticing that Mary was calling. She hardly ever did, so he felt guilty missing her call, but now was not the time.

"Sorry," he apologized. "It's off now."

James didn't know what he'd expected when meeting with the judge, but it wasn't this. He'd had a vague idea that he'd be sitting in a large leather chair surrounded by dark, cherry-stained hardwood bookshelves stuffed with burgundy and gold-trimmed law books. Instead, he was in a simple conference room that looked like it belonged to a seedy accounting firm. The pale gray walls looked like a mixture of leftover paint dumped together and rolled on hastily. He faced a bank of plate glass windows with sun streaming in through lopsided ribbons; it only highlighted the fact that the blinds were badly in need of dusting.

"Was that your girlfriend calling?" the gray- and bushy-haired judge asked.

James blushed, shoved the phone in his pocket, and ignored the question. The judge gave him a smile that was probably meant to put James at ease, but all he could think was how yellow the judge's teeth were compared to the ugly gray walls. Maybe he should just pick a parent or agree to switch off, living a week with one and a week with the other until he left for college. But the thought of living with either of them alone—or worse, with their new significant others, like Mary's dad now had—was more than James could bear. He adjusted his uncomfortable position in the molded plastic orange chair and the metal feet made a blood-curdling screech against the linoleum floor.

The judge acknowledged their surroundings; he didn't exactly apologize for their meeting place, but explained that since Monday was Memorial Day, he was going to the lake with his family and this was the only time and place they could meet. And his office was being remodeled.

"I know your life lately—and probably for quite some time—has revolved around your parents' separation and divorce. But we're here to focus on you. We want to find the best arrangement for you. So please consider me your advocate and answer the questions as honestly as you can." He flashed a smile, but James felt like just another case and sensed the smile was part of the script. "It's not a test and don't worry about hurting anyone's feelings."

"I already know what I want," James said.

"Then this should be easy," grinned the judge.

Easy?! James wanted to scream.

"Why don't you tell me which parent you'd like to live with and I'll ask you some questions about the pros and cons."

"I don't want to live with either one of them. I'm tired of being used by them as a pawn or a weapon to hurt each other. I want to live with my Aunt Row."

The judge's bushy eyebrows furrowed and he scribbled some notes. "I see. What's your aunt's full name? And where does she live?"

"Rowena Nolan. And she only lives a few miles from our— from Mom's—place."

"I'll be! Rowena Nolan! Why, I remember Row. We went to a few dances together back in the day."

James again shifted uncomfortably in his chair. He didn't like the thought of his Aunt Row with His Honor.

"If I recall, there was a fella fighting for her, told me to back off. One of the reasons I became a lawyer and a judge, actually. I didn't like being pushed around." The slight pause indicated it was an attempt at humor, but James wasn't in the mood to chuckle. "Whatever happened to Row, then? Did she marry the devil?"

"I don't—no, she never—" James didn't like this conversation. It was none of the judge's business, unless, of course it related to James's case; but James could see that it didn't. (He now also had some more questions for Aunt Row, but that was for another time.) "So how does it work? How do I get to live with her?"

"Well, ideally, the court likes to see your parents have joint custody. The preference is for a healthy relationship with both parents."

"Yes, but what if that's not healthy?"

The judge displayed a sympathy simper and his tone bordered on condescending. "In case we need a backup plan, though, can you see living with one parent over another, or living with both of them alternately?"

"I don't have a backup. I want to live with Aunt Row."

James resolved he didn't care what the court decided; he was moving in with Aunt Row whether his parents, the bushy-haired judge, or the court approved or not. He just hoped Aunt Row would go for it. And the sooner the better. He wondered now how long he'd have to wait if the judge was going on vacation.

When he got in his car to head for Bev's game, figuring he'd get there around the third or fourth inning, he turned his phone back on. Four messages from Mary. They had gone to see Twig without him, she'd said, but she had wanted to be sure to keep him "in orbit." His heart kicked against his ribs double-time. "No!" he yelled at the messages. He'd wanted to go with her; he'd done all the prep work with Twig, after all. He'd wanted to ask the follow-up questions.

James called Mary back, but there was no answer, as was often the case. She still didn't grasp the concept of cell phones. At least she'd tried to call him four times. Well, now he'd have to go see her and the rest of the group in person—just like the old days before cell phones—to find out what had gone down with Twigler.

20

Broken Record

An exhausted Bev draped her sweaty self over her friends as they smothered her with accolades after the tournament finally ended late in the day on Saturday. The physical exertion of four games in the last two days, coupled with her roller coaster ride of emotions from anger at Conrad to disdain of Diane and the need to rally to a positive attitude, left her limp and drained. But there was an overall glow of happiness for having accomplished what she set out to do: win some games and impress the scouts.

"Food?" Mary laughed, poking Bev in the ribs.

"Food would be . . . *epic*," Bev said, quoting one of Carla DiFrancisco's favorite words. The Fifties Chix laughed.

"We have to update you on what happened with Twig this morning," Mary said.

"Whatever there is to update," Ann muttered. Ann had been slightly less cheerful than her normal self, the others couldn't help but notice.

"And I'm driving because I want the update, too," said James, approaching Bev, Maxine, Mary, Judy, and Ann. "The diner?"

"Where else?" laughed Judy.

They started off together when Diane Dunkelman strutted over. "Hey," she said in her usual demanding tone.

The girls and James stopped and turned to her, no one quite wanting to hear what she had to say.

"You." She pointed at Bev. "Good games. And you." She pointed at Maxine. "I'm sorry for my lame joke."

"Thanks," Bev and Maxine said in unison, then looked at each other and chuckled. Diane waved goodbye but Maxine stopped her. "Diane? Do you and your friends want to join us for a malt?"

"Join us and Bob," Judy piped up. Eyes turned to Judy. "I texted him," she said, shrugging with an impish smile.

"What the heck," sighed Diane. "Yo, DiFran and Lacy; we're going with the Fifties Chix! To—where?" she turned back to ask.

"The fifties diner in Clayton," Bev said.

"Of course. A fifties diner. Where else?" Diane rolled her eyes.

Dear Diary,   29th of May

Bev is a real star athlete! We spent most of the day watching her play, and though I'm not very knowledgeable about sports, I got an education watching her. Not only did I learn about softball (and baseball for her other games), I learned how she keeps her cool in stressful situations, like when the bases are loaded and her team is already behind a run (not a point, a run, James corrected me). I learned what a good leader she is for her team, and for us when we pay attention.

Before her tournament, we went to see Mr. Twigler, the custodian that James interviewed. During this whole experience, I've felt scared, elated, hopeful, and despondent; but being at his house was the first time I've felt spooked. We went to ask him questions in the guise of the "This is Your Life" retrospective for Mrs. F, but really it's because James thinks—and we all agree—that he knows something about time travel and our predicament specifically. We didn't get the answers we want, not even close, but I feel like we are on to something. And we did find out that Mrs. F's and Aunt Row's best friend, Emily Jackson, left suddenly. That was the spookiest part.

Tomorrow the five of us are all going to visit Mr. Fairview. Maybe he'll have some pictures and funny stories we can use for Mrs. F's tribute. And more importantly, maybe he'll have some answers for us. He is, after all, the love of Mrs. F's life and knows her better than anybody!

Always,

Mary

PS—James is a sweetheart. I didn't think I could like him more than I did, but I do. He seems preoccupied, though. I have to remember that there is life going on outside my little world!

Dear Diary,   May 29
     Bob and I are on texting terms now! If
you don't know what that means, don't
worry. I'm only just learning about it
myself. Now that I have a cellular telephone,
I'm learning that I can use it for more
than just talking...I can type on it and send
a typed message to Bob's phone! I really like
talking to him more, though. And a lot of
times, like his instant messages online, I
don't understand the words that he is
typing to me. But the important thing is:
he is typing to me!!
     Well, today, he had games the same time as
Bev (because she played for the girls' softball
team today and they won and she is going to
play around the world on a special team for
girls!!) and Bob's team won its games which
means they are the absolute best in the
entire state of Missouri! I'm so proud of
him, even though I didn't get to see him play.
But even better, Diary, when all of us Chix
went to the diner after Bev's games,

Conrad, Maxine's cousin, and Gary and Bob came and joined us. I invited Bob by a typed text message—and OK, Diane was there, but he didn't pay as much attention to her as he did to me! Boy, was she frosted about that. But her dad showed up at her last game, so she was in a better mood than I've seen her in a long time.

I told Bob that I am going to audition for the summer play, and just like I knew he would be, he was impressed. Just wait until I get the lead! He'll be in the front row watching me on Opening Night and he'll be sighing, "Diane who?"

Love,
Judy White Jenkins

Saturday, May 29 –
· Well this will be a day that goes down in "famy." (The opposite of infamy.) Bev got Diane Dunkelman reinstated to the softball team for their tournament. At first, I was

tempted to be so hurt. But I trust Bev, so
I let it "play out" (I'm fracturing myself
today! I'm so funny!) and when the games
were over, without any teacher or principal or
coach or parent telling her she had to, Diane
apologized to me..

   I understand why Dr. King called forgiveness "a process of life" and a "weapon of
social redemption," and why he said "forgiveness is the solution to the race problem." I
wonder if I hadn't forgiven Diane before she'd
apologized if she still would have said sorry?
Perhaps. But if she had apologized and I
hadn't been ready for it, I would still be in
bondage to my own animosity.

   My hope now is for everyone I love to
know the freedom that comes with
forgiveness.
Maxine

WE ARE STATE CHAMPIONS!! Not that I got to play. I told Coach Raz that I wanted to play with the softball team, even though it's not their regular season. Scouts came to recruit for a national team! And guess who got on? That's right, Diane Dunkelman. Ha! Also, yours truly. I guess I can't escape her because we'll be playing together. AGAIN. It won't be <u>that</u> bad.

Here are my stats for last night's baseball game and today's tourney of three softball games:

PITCHING	HITTING
Innings pitched: 22	At bats: 15
Strikeouts: 21	Runs: 6
Walks: 10	Hits: 5
ERA: 3.0	RBIs: 8
	Batting Average: .331

Coach Raz said I broke two school records. One, I'm the only person to hit home runs on the softball and baseball teams during the same season (that's not official because it's not official softball season, though). And two, the home run I hit last night was the longest one ever hit by a pitcher.

Other stats:
Conrad came to the diner with Bob after their games. They were in a good mood, I guess, because they both forgave me for playing with the girls. Conrad said, "I really liked hanging out with you last night. Think we can do that again sometime?"
I said, "We are right now."
And he said, "I mean just the two of us."
I felt all warm, like my hand did when he was holding it in my dream.
"Now that baseball is done, I'll have lots of free time," I said.

~~I hate~~
I like
I really really like
I love Conrad Marshall!!!

- Bev

Dear Irina,   29 May

   I feel ashamed to admit this to you, but I was jealous when Gary Jenkins and you were emailing each other. I know it sounds awful, and it's not that I didn't trust you, it's just that I was beginning to think I might like him and I wasn't ready to share him. He kept talking about you in glowing terms, which I understand. See, I wasn't quite ready to share you, either!

   Well, friends and I went to dinner together and he showed up. He sat right next to me and we talked and he said he found you very interesting, but that he found me more interesting. It was apparent that the main reason he was in contact with you was to find out more about me. But I guess you know that! So, tonight, I will keep it short because all I really want to say is "Thank you." And I hope you two will stay friends.

   And I think I'd like to learn how to use the computer to have a video call with you.

   Your Cousin Always,
   ☙—Ann

Epilogue

The timing couldn't have been worse. Reginald Fairview had been cherry-picking letters from his fiancée's secret personal collection, had found the five class assignments from the girls at her school and confiscated those, and now, when he needed it most, the watch was missing. May had stopped wearing it, so his plan of offering to take it and have it cleaned for her to wear on their wedding day was dashed. Maybe it was for the best; they would be married in a couple of weeks and they could live a normal life together. So what if he lost money—a lot of money— on this investment? So what if he had to go back to working for one of his father's subsidiaries? If his new company contracting for the government had gone forward, he'd certainly have to tell Marion what he'd been up to and she would feel betrayed. How could she not?

He had his answer about whether or not to move forward with the FairView Project when he was on his way up the stairs of the Nolans' garage apartment to take Marion out for one of their last dates as a couple of engaged kids. He grabbed the mail that Mrs. Nolan had put in a basket at the base of the staircase for her tenant and flipped through the posted items, knowing he shouldn't, but *thinking what did it matter since in just a few weeks they'd be sharing mail anyway.*

He froze on the third step when he spotted the envelope and sender. Then, mindful that he could be seen from the Nolans' house and from Marion's apartment windows, he continued jauntily up the steps while surreptitiously slipping the letter into his sport coat pocket, the one that had already secretly transported so many letters that weren't meant for his eyes.

Though May was up for a movie after dinner and tried to convince him to take her to see the new Walt Disney cartoon Lady and the Tramp, *Reggie feigned fatigue and called it a night. He wasn't sure how he pulled off seeming tired; his nerves felt like snipped live wires, he was so wide awake with anticipation of reading the letter.*

He didn't wait to get home. After dropping Marion off and turning the first corner he came to, he pulled the car to the curb, cut the gas, flicked his lighter to ignite a cigarette, and kept the lighter open to read the letter by in the darkening purple summer twilight.

New Orleans, Louisiana
June 1955

Dear May and Row,
    I hope you are reading this and haven't taken a flame to the envelope upon seeing my name. I would not be surprised if you couldn't forgive me for leaving you with no explanation. I pray it is not too late to give you one.

First, I hope my note finds you well. Please know that I miss you both. Not a day goes by that I don't think of you and our adventures in St. Louis . . . during both wars. I wouldn't blame you if you never thought of me. But I know you well — I feel that even ten years later — and I don't think you'd have a malicious thought about anyone, even me.

I have a sister, girls. My grandparents kept from me that I have a sister, Viola, who survived the accident with my parents. When I found out that she had been given away, I simply had to find her. At the time, I couldn't imagine anyone understanding my heritage but her. But now I know, as lovely as she is — for I have found her! — that you have understood all along. You were with me at the Dunkelman plantation and met my great-grandfather when he was a baby; you were with me on the Underground Railroad; you met my ancestors and Viola never did.

I want to come home. I have opened a dance studio in New Orleans where my sister and her adopted parents live, but I can teach dance in St. Louis. I am writing to ask if you will take me back in; if my two grandest friends in the world will forgive me, I will move with Viola, who also has family in St. Louis, and start fresh. I want the three of you to meet; I know you will get along smashingly well.

If I don't hear from you, I understand that the answer is no. I understand that you need your space and have continued in your lives without me. I do hope that there is room for me.

Your friend forever,
Emily

Reggie switched the lighter off, the image of the flickering flame a scar wherever his gaze rested. A roar filled his ears like an ocean tide with no ebb. He couldn't blame the cicadas in the trees above the car for the racket; it was the adrenaline coursing through him, the fear, thrill, and exhilaration of knowing that he was about to change history. It was no longer an option; there was no denying that the tech-

nology was possible and it would be flat-out irresponsible if he didn't develop it for the good of his country and all mankind.

He folded the letter, replacing it in the envelope and tucking it back into his jacket pocket. He could never let Marion see the letter; he'd returned the others, but this one scared him. What if Emily came back and Marion time-traveled with her right out of his life, depriving him of both his bride and his livelihood? He put his shaking hands on the wheel to steady them. He couldn't drive, not yet.

His heart raced. He would do something with his family's money . . . . He would make his own fortune and he would leave his mark on the world the way no one in history had ever done before.

"Please forgive me, May." He prayed silently for that moment in the future when he admitted to her what he was going to do. "And thank you."

Yes, Reginald Fairview was on the brink of greatness and he had Marion Boggs to thank for it.

Glossary

Balkan Wars/Yugoslav Wars: The Balkan Peninsula is in southeastern Europe, surrounded by water on three sides and very mountainous. It consists of twelve regions and used to be known as the Yugoslav Republic. In the first half of the twentieth century, the region suffered through the Balkan Wars and World War II. In the 1990s, a series of wars and civil wars broke out among several of the regions who wanted greater autonomy when Slovenia and Croatia declared their independence from a central government in Belgrade, Yugoslavia. The War in Slovenia (1991), Croatian War of Independence (1991–1995), Bosnian War (1992–1995), and Kosovo War (1998–1999; included the NATO bombing of Yugoslavia where Ann's mother was lost) constitute the "Yugoslav Wars." Eventually the republics declared independence, but for a decade, there was a great deal of violence and unrest (which included extensive ethnic cleansing) that historians say was the deadliest conflict since World War II. The dissolution of Yugoslavia resulted in six sovereign republics: Slovenia, Croatia, Bosnia and Herzegovina, Macedonia, Montenegro, and Serbia.

Belgrade, Yugoslavia: located in what is now Serbia, the beautiful capital of the former Yugoslavia and the largest city in the country. "Belgrade" means White City and is at the confluence of the Danube and Sava rivers.

Broken record: Instead of CDs or iTunes files, and even before cassettes, music was recorded onto vinyl disks called records. There were three different speeds on which the records played, depending on the size of the record: a whole (double-sided) record or LP ("Long Play") played at 33, a single song (which had a flip side with one song) played at 45 (so the singles were referred to as 45s), and the even older records played at 78. Because the vinyl could be easily scratched, the records would often "skip" or get stuck in the same groove, repeating the same part over and over again. So "broken record" refers to hearing or saying the same thing over and over again.

Cast an eyeball: watch, look at

Cat-eye glasses: glasses that are shaped like cats' eyes, with pointed frames

Cloud nine: the best, your happy place

Clutched: DE-nied! Turned down, rejected

Drag: bummer

Earthbound: reliable, dependable, predictable

Ethnic Cleansing: "The process or policy of eliminating unwanted ethnic or religious groups by deportation, forcible displacement, mass murder, or by threats of such acts, with the intent of creating a territory inhabited by people of a homogeneous or pure ethnicity, religion, culture, and history." —Wikipedia.com

Fracture: to amuse to no end

Fream: a freak or misfit

Frosted: angry

Put down: an insult, an intentional slight

Rollers: Before flat irons, curling irons, and hand-held hair dryers, many girls and women put their hair in curlers or rollers every night, put a sleeping cap on over it, and slept that way.

Slobodan Milošević: communist leader in the 1980s and 1990s in Yugoslavia whose goal was to build a Greater Serbia. Known for the "ethnic cleansing" and crimes he perpetrated against ethnic Albanians (Bosnians, Croats, Muslims, and non-Serbs), he was arrested for sixty-six war crimes in 1999, but maintained his innocence.

BE KEPT IN ORBIT, HEP CATS!

Look for these other titles in the Fifties Chix series:

Book 1: Travel to Tomorrow

Book 2: Keeping Secrets

Book 3: Third Time's a Charm

Book 5: Till the End of Time

Check out **www.FiftiesChix.com** and join the Fan Club for updates on the Fifties Chix book series, more info on your fave characters, secret diary entries, contests, and more!

Also visit the Fifties Chix wiki at

http://fiftieschix.wikispaces.com

for extended activities and fun educational stuff.

BOOK 1

1950 1960 1970 1980 *FiftiesChix* 1990 2000 2010 2020

travel to tomorrow

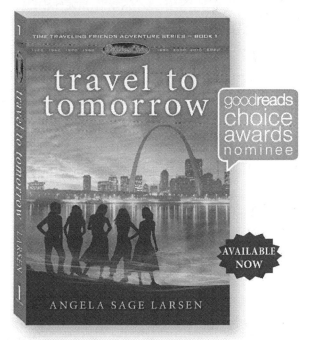

Sock hops. Soda fountains. Slumber parties. Life in 1955 is simple for tomboy Beverly, moody Maxine, high-spirited Judy, studious Mary and artistic Ann. But after a class assignment to predict life in the future, they wake up the next morning in a future they could never have imagined (having time-traveled into a parallel universe to the 21st century. With only each other to trust, they must work together and find their way "home" to 1955; but the more they discover about the future, will they even want to go back?

SIGN UP TO GET UPDATES AND READ SNEAK PREVIEWS OF UPCOMING BOOKS AT FIFTIESCHIX.COM

BOOK 2

1950 1960 1970 1980 *Fifties Chix* 1990 2000 2010 2020

keeping secrets

THE MYSTERY UNFOLDS IN A FUTURE LINKED TO THE PAST
THROUGH SECRETS THAT MUST NOW BE UNCOVERED AND TOLD.

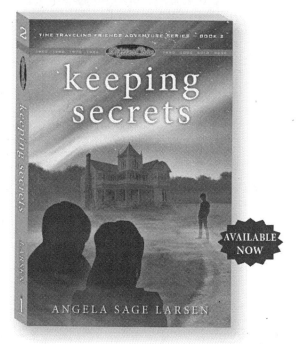

As if their quest to return home isn't challenging enough for Fifties Chix friends Mary, Ann, Judy, Maxine, and Bev – they must also cope with a love triangle between Mary, Ann and James O'Grady; the unexplained disappearance of their classroom teacher; and the revealing essay Maxine writes for the school's underground newspaper.

Hang on tight as the time-traveling quintet explodes through well-kept secrets to find the answers in the second book of the Fifties Chix series.

BOOK 3

1950 1960 1970 1980 *Fifties Chix* 1990 2000 2010 2020

third time's a charm

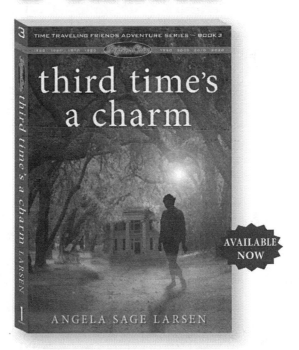

In 1945 May Boggs, the Fifties Chix' social studies teacher, is 15 years old. World War II has taken its toll and May and her two best friends, Rowena and Emily, are happy to see the war coming to an end at long last. But their bright futures are disrupted by a trip back to another war torn era – the Civil War.

When in modern day, Maxine pays the price for the controversial essay she wrote for the school's underground paper, the secret her teacher uncovers in 1864 may be the very thing that saves Maxine's – and the Fifties Chix' – reputation and future.

SIGN UP TO GET UPDATES AND READ SNEAK PREVIEWS OF UPCOMING BOOKS AT FIFTIESCHIX.COM

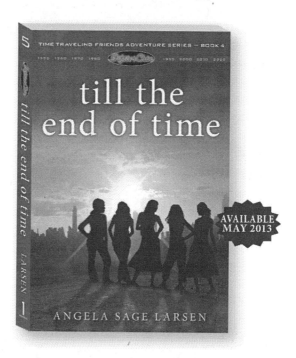